I0672069

Noah's Ark

C. J. Korryn

Published by C. J. Korryn Books
2018

Published by:

C. J. Korryn Books

First Edition ©2018 by C. J. Korryn

Visit C. J. Korryn's website below

for more of his books.

https://www.cjkorryn.com/books

Sign up for C.J. Korryn's

newsletter

https://authorcjkorryn.wixsite.com/mailinglist

Contents

INTRODUCTION

In ages past and ancient times, days of old, and long since forgotten, the known world died and birthed anew, its inhabitants, save one heroic family, annihilated.

The world long ago was a much different world without day and night as we know them today, a world with a firmament that shone a brilliant pink glow that rolled over the daytime sky as the sun crept along above. The night was a faint pink glistening hue of stars as they sparkled like glitter. The moon was a red ruby hanging in the night sky. The world's terrain of diverse vegetation was peaceful. Its calm glasslike streams and lakes, and its ocean (for in those days stood a single enormous land mass) stood as quiet and smooth as a mirror's surface.

It was a world where animals roamed freely, out in the open wilds in perfect harmony with one another; for back in the old world, meat was not eaten, nor were the animals vicious creatures. Man and beast were kindred spirits...for a time.

Man soon grew vile and wicked, consumed with evil. Chaotic and cruel, they killed for the simple pleasure of seeing the creatures of the old world suffer and die. Drunkards and brawlers killed for money, women, and sport. An evil race, once pure, became unholy, a disgrace to their Creator, the very one who birthed their existence.

FAMILY

Noah sat on the edge of a small cliffside overlooking Fulstron, the great city in which he lived near the outskirts. Noah often came there to think and meditate. It was by far his favorite place to relax. He looked over the many lanterns burning throughout the city. It seemed to Noah the tiny flickers from the many torches in the town were almost a mirror image of the peaceful, glistening pink stars in the night sky. From this vantage point up in the cliffs it truly seemed Fulstron was a magnificent town. Its sparkling fires were a peaceful dance of beauty. He knew, however, the realities of Fulstron, a dangerous and evil city at night, and not much safer in the daylight.

It was just before dawn, and he could see the rolling cloud of daylight climbing up behind the city consuming the sparkling stars as it rose into the sky. Noah always loved watching the sunrise. He loved the change that seemed to happen so quickly. The sun turned the dim light of the stars and moon into the brightly shining sunlight as it peeked up into the horizon, bringing the dull colors of the limited view of the night into the vibrant colors of the daytime. It seemed almost that God himself was repainting the world anew each day.

A gush of wind suddenly breezed by, blowing his dark brown hair into his deep brown eyes as the sunlight fell upon him from the edges of the horizon, warming his dark tanned skin. He could always feel the sudden change in temperature when the sun came up. It was so extreme and reminded him again of the dramatic change of the night and day. He stood to his feet, brushing off the dirt from his brown leggings and started his hike back down into the valley to his shop just inside the town walls, his brown lace-up shirt blowing wildly in the warming air of the cliffside.

Later that day, Noah sat in his workshop studying sketches for his next project, a large bench piece that called for ornate carvings throughout the bench itself—truly a test of skill for this master carpenter! He heard a commotion outside and peered out the window. It didn't surprise him when he saw two swordsmen battling—it happened all the time in this city. He recognized one of the two as Ephron: a soon-to-be-wed bachelor. The other he knew as the self-proclaimed best swordsmen of Fulstron. Perez: older than Ephron and more experienced with the way of the sword, had long since claimed to be the best. The young Ephron, with his followers, had argued otherwise—and they were now settling the dispute. Noah watched as the two fought for several minutes and scanned the streets for any signs of the city guard to stop the fight. The guards only showed up just in time to see the crowd dwindling down and the young Ephron with a hole in his gut, dying. Noah soon returned to his work, working for several more hours on the bench. It was hard work, but there was nothing in the world Noah loved more than working with wood, forming it and shaping it into something great. He felt at ease with it as he worked, almost as if it was part of him, an extension of himself. Indeed, it was an extension of his creativeness, of his mind's eye. Noah could make almost anything. All he had to do was picture it in his mind, and it was as if the wood just began to shape itself. He had often wondered how he had finished many of his projects; for it seemed that when he had just started, he began his finishing touches. Lost somewhere between time and his woodwork he rarely recalled actually working on the pieces. When he worked on his wood, he left this world behind and ventured into a world all his own. He loved what he did, and he lived to do what he did.

Night fell, and still, Noah worked. It was only when he noticed a familiar sweet smell that he stopped to realize the sun had gone down...and his wife standing a few feet in front of him with a picnic basket in hand. Suddenly, his stomach sank, and his chisel fell from his hand, clanging on the wood floor as he realized the time.

"I thought I would find you here," his dark-skinned wife said with a smile that spread from cheek to cheek, contrasting with Noah's face of dread upon noticing his wife and suddenly remembering he was supposed to meet her for their three-hundred fiftieth anniversary (man lived much, much longer then, and Noah was yet a middle-aged man). Naomi's own face quickly faded as she realized her husband's despair.

"I am a wretched husband!" he said, at last, his voice filled with shame. Naomi set the basket on a small table next to her and lovingly took her husband in her arms.

"You are a wonderful and loving husband who cares deeply for his wife...and his work," she replied.

"I should have remembered," he said softly.

"You were too lost in your work to notice if the city were engulfed in fire!" she joked. Noah smiled.

"Indeed, I was blessed from heaven itself to have a wife such as you!"

"Shall we head to Heaven's Ridge?" Naomi asked. Heaven's Ridge had been their traditional anniversary sight since the day Noah had asked her to marry him on that very cliffside. Noah grabbed the picnic basket in one arm and wrapped the other around Naomi's and the two headed for the door. Noah stopped suddenly, staring at several lanterns burning near his workstation. "What? What is it?" Naomi asked, confused.

"I don't even remember lighting the lanterns!" he replied, rushing over to blow them out as they left.

Noah and Naomi strolled down the street, nearing several men making a loud commotion and a dozen onlookers passing by. As the two grew closer, they noticed two men beating a third and spouting off curses. Noah released his arm from around his wife's waist.

"Hold this!" he ordered, handing off the basket, and raced to the aide of the helpless man before Naomi could object.

Noah leaped in with his shoulder leading, smacking hard into the closest of the two men, sending him stumbling sideways into a wall a few feet away. Noah spun around as the second noticed Noah and connected his fist with Noah's cheek. Noah stumbled, as both men advanced, the first swinging for Noah's face, which Noah easily dodged, and the other landing a punch into Noah's ribs. Noah retaliated with a headbutt into the stomach, sending the man stumbling backward clutching his abdomen. The first man grabbed Noah in a bear hug from behind. Noah quickly brought an elbow into his opponent's side and bent low, toppling to the ground in a spin and bringing his attacker under him. Noah elbowed him several more times until he was released, just in time to be kicked in the side of the face, opening a large gash in his cheek. Noah went rolling, blinded by the pain and dazed by the sudden assault on his senses. Noah's attacker hopped over his comrade and advanced toward Noah. Noah quickly spun and brought his legs into his attacker's feet as hard as he could. The man fell hard to his back, smacking his head on the ground, knocking him unconscious as Noah jumped to his feet. Noah's second attacker jumped to his feet as well and charged, bringing another fist into Noah's ribs. Noah saw the hit coming and accepted the harsh blow, bringing his own arm down onto his opponent's forearm, locking it between his ribs and his own arm. He quickly slammed his free elbow into the man's ear, sending him stumbling to the ground. Noticing his counterpart unconscious and himself in a world of hurt, he wanted nothing more to do with this fight and stumbled off into the night.

Several hours later, Noah and Naomi sat in front of their hearth, Naomi cleaning Noah's cheek wound and Noah wincing every time she touched his face.

"So much for our anniversary," Noah said. "I'm sorry. I couldn't let those men just beat that poor man, no matter what he did."

"I know. You did the right thing." From the tone of her voice, Noah knew she was sincere in her thoughts and held no anger toward him for his actions. "I was scared, though, when I saw you went to the ground, and that man kicked you. I thought I would be a widow," she said, a sad smile on her beautiful face. Noah gently rested his hand on her knee, returning an apology-filled smile. He sat quietly for the next few minutes and let Naomi finish; then the two retired for the evening.

***

Ham shifted from shelf to shelf restocking his store. He was tall and lean, though with a noticeable muscular

17

frame, (mostly from lifting heavy objects as he often had to in restocking his shop), with raven black, wavy hair down to his mid-neck. He wore a thin cloth shirt and leggings of dark brown, matching his sandals.

As the owner, he took great pride in taking excellent care of the shop, ensuring it to be the finest store in all of Fulstron and spent hours after the shop closed down cleaning and organizing it. He gently set each item in a perfect row, shelving the newest of his identical pottery pieces to the back and bringing his older to the front, separating them by color, then tallest to shortest. Next, he shifted the one-of-a-kinds from tallest to shortest, again color coordinating them. He continued this process with the various sizes of cooking cauldrons, wash basins and heating pots. Finally finished with the shelves, he moved over to miscellaneous items such as ropes, chains, hunting equipment, traveling equipment; separating them by type, size, weight, length, and craftsmanship. He then moved to the larger cooking cauldrons, bath basins, chairs, tables, desks, beds, and other household items; separating them, again, from largest to smallest, wood type, color, and design. Last, he moved to beddings, linens, fabrics, and furs; separating them from size, cloth material, weave or stitch pattern, the rarity of material, and color. He separated the furs again by size, color, rarity, and fur pattern.

Finally finished, he stood back and examined the newly stocked, and full shop, noticed several items crooked or bent slightly out of alignment, and corrected them instantly, then swept. Finally satisfied, he began his way to the stairs in the back of his shop that led to his office but stopped in stride as he noticed an all-too-familiar scene. Two of the city guards were harassing a fellow townsman, a short, stubby old man with a cane and a limp. Ham stood a moment watching, marveling at the so-called "law enforcement" of his wicked town. The night here seemed to bring out the worst in people, even the more reputable of the large city. The city guards, however, were never known for being reputable or honorable, and even less so during the twisted hours of darkness.

Maybe the darkness harbored some sort of evil spirit, or maybe it was just that the night brought forth and let out the evil that truly lived within man's heart—perhaps both.

The two soldiers quickly stood to attention as a third soldier joined the group. Ham couldn't hear what they were saying, but he knew the soldiers were being harshly scolded, both by the looks on their faces and because Ham recognized this third soldier, a captain by the name of Shem—his brother. He admired his brother; he had to admit. Unlike Ham, Shem had a very noticeable muscular build, dark skin, finely cut short hair that hid under his helmet, and a cleanly shaven face. His eyes, though, held a depth to them that none could really understand. Sunken with an imagined responsibility and stress, he was the sole protector of Fulstron and only righteous guard in all the land. He held to his principles and forced those under his command to comply with them—at least while they were on the job.

The elderly man grabbed his cane and fled as fast as his old body would allow, and once Shem had finished his scolding, the soldiers stood still at attention as Shem glanced toward Ham through the window nodding toward the door. Ham quickly rushed to unlock it and held it open for Shem. Shem wore the same armor as all the soldiers: a bronze breastplate with the city insignia of a bear on it, a sword sheathed in its scabbard, and a bronze helmet. His signifying rank mark, a purple strap on each shoulder, identified him as a unit commander.

"I'll let them stand out there a while," Shem reported as he entered. "Teach them a lesson, maybe." Ham smiled. "You're up late, brother," Shem accused.

"Restocking; just got a new shipment in. A lot of stuff," Ham replied. "Business has been good. Was just about to lock up before I saw that." He finished and pointed to the two guards who still stood perfectly still.

"Well, just thought I would come by. Better finish my rounds and let you get to bed," Shem said and patted his brother on the back. Ham locked the door behind his brother and left for home, chuckling at the thought of seeing the two soldiers still standing outside his window in the morning.

***

Shem strode down the streets patrolling his sector. He had just reprimanded a couple of soldiers for their conduct with a townsman. Almost every night, it seemed, he was scolding one of his seventy-five troops for something! He noticed, several dozen yards away, another pair of his soldiers harassing yet more townsmen. As he neared, he saw they weren't townsmen at all, but townswomen and his soldiers were doing more than harassing them. One soldier had gone so far as to start unlacing one of the women's shirts. The other had his body pressed up against the woman. Shem quickly glanced around, not another soul in sight. Never had he witnessed such a heinous act in the open streets. Of course, who would confront city guards? Likely no one, and if they did, they would probably end up in jail for a crime they didn't commit.

Shem rocketed into a sprint, his eyes burning with fury. He closed the distance in a matter of seconds and came crashing into the first of the soldiers, sending him sprawling to the street with a howl of shock. Shem continued his rush, bringing an elbow into the next man's face as he knocked him to the street with a shout as well. Shem quickly turned again to the first soldier as he began to get up and brought the side of his boot into his face.

"You'd both stay down if you knew what was good for you!" he shouted and turned to the helpless women, who stood shamefully against the wall covering their exposed skin.

The first soldier took Shem's words to heart and lay still on the street covering his bloody face. However, his partner raised to his hand and knees. When Shem noticed this, he brought his foot around smacking the man's arm out from under him, then dropped his foot onto his back, forcing him to stay down.

Several guards rounded the street corners from every direction, their swords drawn, then re-sheathed their weapons upon realizing what had happened.

"Take these two to the prison cells!" ordered Shem. Immediately, three guards hoisted the two beaten soldiers up and escorted them off.

"You two, with me," he ordered pointing to two young guards. "The rest of you get back to work! And don't let me catch you so much as touching any townspeople!" he hollered, irate. He turned to the two young guards.

"We are going to escort these two ladies home, and we will be gentlemen," he spoke angrily, then turned to the two ladies and spoke calmly and gently.

"We will take you home. No harm will come to you. I promise. These two gentlemen will take you by the shoulders, nothing more." He nodded to the guards, and they gingerly put their arms around the women. "Now, tell us where you live." The women pointed straight, still not saying a word. Shem and the two soldiers followed their directions. After a few minutes, the women began giving verbal directions to their homes.

***

Midafternoon, the day after Ham had witnessed his brother scolding a couple of his subordinates, Japheth, his other brother, entered Ham's shop. Ham wasn't in sight, so he quietly made his way down several of the isles adjusting his brother's meticulously organized shelves with a wide grin. He moved a large cooking pot with a row of smaller ones and set a small pot in its place. He carefully set a tall, slender water basin into one of the large wash tubs and ruffled several small animal skins so that they were no longer stacked neatly on top one another. Then he mixed the carefully separated carpets and larger animal skins.

Ham entered from the back room, immediately noticing Japheth with a smirk.

"What are you doing?" he asked accusingly. Japheth, startled at his brother's sudden appearance, replied sarcastically.

"Well, hello to you too big brother." Ham walked over to his little brother, eyeing him suspiciously, noticing the pile of furs in front of him, and hissed in irritation.

"You're always up to something!" he said, frustrated as he fumbled through the skins, re-separating them into their proper piles. "You joke too much. What else did you mess with?" Japheth's smile morphed into a frown.

"Brother, I'm shocked that you would think of me like that," he replied sarcastically. "I touched nothing. You simply caught me when I was rummaging through these fine furs and hadn't the chance to straighten them out again before you came in," he lied.

"I don't believe you for a second. Now, what else have you messed with?"

Japheth simply smiled.

"Are you coming tomorrow night?" he asked.

"Am I going where?" asked Ham.

"Didn't Dinah tell you? I'm having a party celebrating the rise of the new year." Ham rolled his eyes.

"No. She didn't, must have forgot...again. It shouldn't be a problem. We don't have any plans. It's at your place?" Japheth nodded. "I'll remind Dinah about it tonight."

"Good. I'll see you tomorrow, then." With that, he left, hearing his brother holler at him as Ham noticed another disruption to his meticulous order.

***

Shem entered Japs' his brother's clothing store. He had just come from his commanding officers' office, which he had seen after his official paperwork was completed at the end of his shift. Japheth's shop was one of the largest in this section of the city, fully two stories high and as large as two shops.

The first floor held stacks and racks of all sorts of clothing from simple tunics to scarves, gloves, night apparel, and undergarments for both men and women. It contained a vast array of formal wear for special occasions for both men and women.

The second floor consisted of his workspaces and stock rooms where Japheth housed the finished products he personally tailored. Japheth's clothes were expensive, but he was the best in the business.

Shem glanced around, scanning for his youngest brother. After a few minutes, he decided Japheth wasn't in the gallery and began to rifle through some of the clothing racks, awaiting his brother's appearance. Just minutes later, Japheth emerged from the storeroom carrying a finely tailored silk dress. He handed it off to a young woman who thanked him and left.

Japheth caught sight of his brother as he came to stand before him, and the two hugged.

"Sorry I can't come to the year's end party, Jep. This banquet has been in the planning for months, and I'm expected to go," Shem reported, releasing his brother.

"I know. You guys have one every year; I just thought we would invite you in case you got a chance to break free."

"Yeah. Well, hopefully, I can slip out early and make it to yours. I figure if I can make myself seen for a while and make the rounds I may be able to get away with sneaking out of there early."

"Sounds good. Let me go get your orders," Japheth replied and slipped back into the storerooms up the stairs. He returned moments later with a pair of cocktail outfits, a beautiful red dress and a military dress uniform. Japheth held them up for Shem to inspect, who nodded in acceptance.

"They are beautiful," Shem admired. Japheth then vanished into a small room, emerging moments later with items wrapped in thick cloth for protection.

"I'll see you later, tomorrow night, hopefully," Japheth said as he handed over the wrapped garments.

"Right," Shem replied, and with his garments gently draped over his arm, he left, with a final wave goodbye.

***

Zaphira mingled the corners of the crowds, keeping only to those she knew. Her long, straight raven black hair matching her devilish black eyes, and her black dress keeping her complexion from appearing overly dark. She mingled only enough to keep her presence known and often retreated to the corners under pretenses of snatching refreshments and appetizers or refilling them. An occasional friend would wave her over to introduce her to their own group of friends. She would greet them uncomfortably, and as the conversation shifted focus from her, she would vanish into the crowd.

She wouldn't say much upon being introduced to strangers, or for that matter, when she hadn't known the person long. She was a quiet person and kept to herself most of the time. It was times like this that she dreaded. She always made a point to keep the tables full, helping her to stay clear of the crowds.

She noticed Ham and Dinah enter through the open door, and greeted them warmly, taking their coats and hanging them in a closet next to the front door. Ham excused himself to mingle

"How are you doing?" Dinah asked. Zaphira sunk back into the closet, with an audible sigh.

"Ahh, I'm so glad you're here!" she began. "I hardly know any of these people. How can my husband know so many people?"

"Come on; I'll save you from the crowds," Dinah said and nodded. "The key is to always look busy or deep in conversation. Any idle time is time that someone thinks they can grab you, so don't look idle." Dinah led Zaphira to one of the tables and began tutoring her on how to keep from being dragged into the crowds.

Japheth met several more guests near the door with a warm greeting and placed their over-garments into the closet. Japheth mingled into the crowds, between greeting new guests, knowing his wife didn't like crowds or groups until he noticed Zaphira heading to the door again, as she saw his parents enter.

***

Noah and his wife crossed through the entryway to Japheth's home, greeted by his wife, Zaphira.

"Great dress," She praised her mother-in-law upon seeing Naomi wearing the same long black dress as her. Naomi smiled in reply.

"Thank you. Yours isn't so bad either." The two chuckled as Naomi led the way across the threshold.

"Make yourselves at home. Can I take your coat?" she asked Noah, who nodded and slipped out of his coat, handing it to Zaphira. She hung the jacket in the closet with the others and escorted them to the refreshments.

"Ham and Dinah are here. They got here a few minutes ago, and I'm sure you will find somebody you know here," Zaphira said.

A short high-pitched scream suddenly erupted, shattering the harmony of the rumble of voices throughout the room and causing a sudden hush as all eyes focused on the large and not-so-attractive woman who jumped up from the couch, her face contorted in surprise and fear, and those surrounding her all burst into hysterical laughter. Waves of chuckles, giggles and snickers arose as onlookers realized what had just happened. The fat woman, her face still red, snatched up a small toy snake and launched it at Japheth, who stood, clutching his stomach. He was laughing so hard he barely noticed it smack him right in the face.

"I…I'm…ss…sorry…." he began, trying to get his words out between breaths of laughter. "…but…I… it…was so…fun…funny," he finally finished.

After a few more minutes, Japheth and his congregation finally stopped their laughing, and the rest of the partygoers returned to their own private conversations, every once and a while making a reference to the fat woman or Japheth.

Noah and Naomi continued to congregate around the refreshments, snacking on the various items and talking with Zaphira for several more minutes before Japheth broke away from his own circle of friends and greeted his parents.

***

Shem and his wife Mirriam entered the officer's ball.

"We'll just talk to as many people as we can for just a few hours; then we'll sneak outta' here.... Deal?" His wife nodded her head as they merged into the crowds and mingled among fellow officers and their wives. Mirriam held herself tall, her shoulders back and head high. She was not the most beautiful woman, more average looking in appearance. However, her proud stature and self-confidence only heightened her beauty. She had long, wavy, brown hair with matching eyes just a few shades lighter, and she wore a formal red dress accented with an expensive diamond necklace and earrings.

Shem wore an all-white, formal jacket with matching pants and shirt. Even his shoes were white, with the only exceptions being the solid black bowtie and his purple strap around his shoulders signifying his rank. It was the standard military attire for such occasions. Shem casually scanned the ballroom on occasion, noting who of importance was there, his sunken eyes darting here and there for just an instant and back to whomever he was in conversation with so he still appeared to be listening to the conversations.

Shem had become an expert in appearing to be interested in whatever his counterparts conversed about while keeping track of those he needed to make an appearance to at these types of events. His wife kept the conversations going along at a reasonable speed, answering questions for him and bringing him back into the conversations with an occasional comment to him directly. They made a good team.

Once Shem found his newest "target," he quickly maneuvered the conversation to a point where he could excuse himself and his wife, and they would move on to the next conversation. They did this several times, then took to the dance floor for a dance or two, knowing they would be seen on the dance floor, and then returned to mingling with those who mattered.

Finally, close to the year's end, they slipped out and headed for Japheth's party. They had always hated these types of events, but as an officer in his position it was a necessary evil, he thought. He knew he wasn't liked much by his leadership, and he had only gotten as far in his career as he had by his impeccable record, and no one had any grounds not to promote him through the ranks. He also knew it looked good for him to go to these events. He could play the game!

They left unnoticed and quietly marched down the dark streets arm in arm. Quickly greeted by a soldier in an alley, who promptly came to attention nervously as he noticed Shem pass by. Shem saw his nervousness and eyed him suspiciously as he passed. He glanced back after a few paces seeing the soldier had vanished. Against his better judgment, Shem continued toward Japheth's house, gritting his teeth against the uneasy sensation that the soldier was up to no good. Being off duty, however, he had no authority over the man, and he knew nothing would come of it if he had caught him doing anything of poor conduct as a guard!

He kept walking, pulling his wife close.

***

The night grew late, and the year's end was nearing. Japheth and Zaphira brought out the traditional wine for the celebration and began passing out goblets. They both noticed Shem and Mirriam slip into the house, and Japheth handed them goblets with a greeting. After returning the

38

unused goblets back to the kitchen, Japheth emerged, tapping his glass to get everybody's attention. The guests quieted, and he began.

"Well everybody, the year's end approaches, and we're all another year older. This year has had its good moments and its bad. It's not-so-fun moments and its fun moment," he raised his glass toward the fat woman. "and its classically embarrassing moments, eh Mariah?"

"No thanks to you, Jep!" she replied, provoking a short chuckle from several of the audience and a sly smile from Japheth.

"May the newest year be full and hopefully not our last!" he raised his glass. "Happy years' end!" he blustered, and the crowd echoed.

***

A lone woman rushed along the dark street. She was on her way to work, and late at that. Her normal travel companions had already left without her, and she knew it

39

was dangerous to venture out at night alone. She was by no means pretty, but she had many curves and a slender figure. She only prayed she wouldn't run into any straggling men this night. She would never have been caught out alone except that she was a single parent and needed the money. She couldn't afford to lose even a day's wages. So, she took her chances.

She rounded the corner in a rush, slamming right into two patrolling guards. The two soldiers stumbled a step back in surprise as the woman let out a startled shriek, then upon realizing whom it was, apologized profusely as she tried to slip past them.

"Hold on there, lass," ordered one of the patrolmen, eying her up and down. "Where you going in such a hurry?" he asked. She stopped, suddenly nervous.

"Work, sir," she replied.

"Don't you know it's not safe out here at night?" the other informed her.

"Yes sir," she answered, her voice shaking, "I'm just going around the corner." The two soldiers glanced up at each other, and the woman noticed something in their eyes. She quickly turned, hoping to get out of arm's reach. One of the soldiers grabbed her.

"Hold on there," he said, his voice taking on a sudden animalistic tone, as the other officer glared up and down the street. She started to scream, and he pulled her tight into him, covering her mouth and muffling the scream. Terror struck her, suddenly, then, and she began to cry, struggling against the soldier's grip. He dragged her into a dark alley just before the next street and slammed her hard against the wall. The other patrolman stood at the entrance to the alleyway.

Two figures emerged from the building at the end of the street and passed by then. The soldier in the ally with the woman held her mouth tight.

"Scream, and I'll kill you," he threatened as he noticed his partner stand at attention. Moments later, the couple passed, and his partner took refuge in the darkness of the alleyway.

***

"Starting off the new year on the right foot, eh brother: late to your own brother's party!" Japheth exclaimed jokingly. Shem smirked in reply.

"Well, just be happy we came at all," he replied in jest. Japheth chuckled.

"We're winding down here, and all the jokes have already been made, but come finish up all the appetizers," he paused, "and we'll need help cleaning this mess up." Again, he got a smirk for a reply.

Japheth was right, the party dwindled to almost nothing shortly after Shem, and Mirriam arrived. Soon after that, it was just the family. They all sat around for a while enjoying each other's company and then they all helped clean up the aftermath of the party. Japheth and Zaphira refused to allow them at first, insisting they wouldn't be good hosts if they let their guests clean, but after the persistence of the family, they relented.

After the cleaning was finished, the family ended the night with wishes for a blessed new year and prosperous year to come.

***

Japheth strolled down the street, toward his home. He had stayed at work a little later than usual after closing his shop to work on some alterations for a customer who was coming by in the morning for a pick up.

The bright pink sky of the day was starting to fade into the pink glow of the moonlit night sky as dusk began to fall.

He knew it wasn't entirely safe in this part of town to travel alone at night, but he sometimes took that chance anyway. He was late for his dinner date with his wife, and he was in a rush. He could have easily skirted the rough area of town and traveled down one of the safer routes, but that would cost him a good twenty minutes at least. So, he decided to chance the rough streets. So far, he hadn't had any trouble on the occasions that he had decided to take this street, except once, when he noticed a pair of strangers following him. Happenstance had it that a couple of patrol officers had taken their route a few minutes early, thus saved him from a mugging, or worse.

Japheth, like the rest of his family, didn't believe in swords—except Shem, but that was, in fact, his job to carry a sword and protect people. Japheth did, however, keep a short wooden truncheon hidden under his garments tonight, just in case he needed to defend himself.

He rounded a corner and noticed a commotion. Several patrons of one of the local pub and gambling establishments gathered just outside the entrance, yelling and screaming. He couldn't make out what they were saying, but he could tell it wasn't pleasant.

As he neared, he could make out more and more of what was happening. He was planning on skirting the crowd, but he noticed what looked like someone hunched over in the middle of the mob.

The moment he realized what was happening his heart leaped out of his chest, and his mind flooded with all the possibilities that could happen in the next few minutes. Seconds later, he darted for the mob, pulling out his small club and started shouting.

He knew it wasn't the smartest thing to do. He knew he should find a patrol, but that would take too long. Of all the thousand possibilities that ran through his head in those few seconds, none of them ended well for the man, nor him. He knew it wasn't the wise thing to do, nor was it a safe thing to do, but....it *was* the *right* thing to do, no matter what.

He screamed for the crowd to stop, as loud as he could, but his voice was drowned out by the angry screams of the mob. He didn't bother to count them, but he knew there were at least half a dozen. He knew it was a futile battle, but he had to try. He just couldn't watch or stand by and do nothing as someone was being beaten to a bloody pulp. Moments later, he reached the first of the men in the mob and smashed the short staff into the back of the guy's knee. The man fell to the ground in a loud scream, grabbing the arms of the two closest men to him. The two turned to see why their counterpart was pulling on them, immediately seeing Japheth. Japheth stabbed his makeshift club into the stomach of the closer of the two, as they turned. The man doubled over in pain as Japheth barreled his shoulder into the other. The two went stumbling sideways into the rest of the mob. Japheth felt a jab to his side as one of his victims screamed a curse. A hand grabbed Japheth and ripped him from the man he had just barreled into. Japheth swung his club back behind him as he twisted out of the hold, landing his blow on his attacker's forearm.

The man yelled in pain. Three more hands grabbed him, and he felt two more punches to the gut. Then he was thrown to the floor. He felt foot after foot kicking him. He covered his face and curled up into a ball to try to shield himself from the kicks. The next few moments he felt nothing but pain, then things started to go numb. He didn't know how long they had been kicking him, and he was on the brink of unconsciousness when they stopped. Then he felt two pairs of hands lift him up. He saw the uniforms of two soldiers scowling at him, and then all went black.

Japheth lurched awake to a bucket of cold water in the face. He immediately felt the throbbing pain in his eye, and cheek, as well as ribs, and he moaned.

"Tough night, brother? Anything broken?" he heard Shem's voice ask, and it was then that he realized where he was. The room was dark and cold. He lay on his back on a solid concrete floor. The walls around him were stone, and it smelled of mildew mixed with human feces and body odor, and the slightest noise echoed. He was in the city jail or dungeon as many called it. It was, by far, the most unpleasant place to be—and Japheth now understood that from first-hand experience.

He sat up slowly, turning his head to look at his brother, who stood just inside the open cell door with a scowl on his face and bucket in hand.

"Thanks for the bath, brother. No, nothing's broken, but *everything* hurts," he replied and noticed a quick smirk flash across Shem's face. Shem extended a hand as he stepped to Japheth's side. Japheth took his hand and pulled himself up.

"What happened last night?"

Japheth stretched his body, cringing at the shooting pain that erupted from his torso.

"I got the crap kicked out of me," he reported.

"I know that," Shem replied irritated. "I mean why did you get involved with that mob? Thankfully, a patrol saw you get beat down by the mob and stopped it before you got seriously hurt."

"I'm surprised they stopped at all," Japheth replied.

"Well, if they hadn't, who knows how bad that mob would have beaten you. How did you get involved in that anyway?"

"I was taking the shortcut home and saw the mob beating some guy, so I tried to stop it."

"By getting *yourself* beat? You shouldn't have gotten involved."

"And, what, just walk by and let the guy be beaten to death?"

"You could have found a patrol. After all, it is *our* job to keep the peace."

"Shem, you know they wouldn't have done anything. The only reason they broke up the mob in the first place was because they know I am your brother. Most of the soldiers cause more disturbance than peace," Japheth retorted angrily.

Shem didn't reply. He knew there was truth in what his brother was saying.

"Well," he said finally, "I have to go. Don't get into trouble on your way home, and your wife is worried sick about you." Japheth nodded as Shem left the confines of the dark, dank cell. Moments later, another soldier emerged from the shadows and nodded for Japheth to follow. The soldier escorted him out, not saying a word. Japheth wondered if the soldier was quiet because he had heard the whole conversation about how corrupt the guards were or if it was something else.

The walk only took a couple of minutes, but those minutes filled with silence seemed longer than they were to Japheth.

The soldier finally led him to the door and opened it. The bright morning pink light and fresh air swept into the dank hallway, unbridled, and overwhelmed his senses. The air careened into his nose, arresting him with the distinct earthy smell of grass and dirt, and the light scorched his vision with piercing, blinding rays. The soldier stepped aside, and Japheth exited into a large open courtyard. To one side stood the command barracks and to the other, the armory and assembly hall. Ahead several yards was the yard entrance, with two guards posted. The yard itself was dirt and short, trampled grass. Here and there, soldiers trained. Japheth casually strolled to the compound exit, and as he approached, the guards opened the gate.

***

Shem stood at attention in front of his commanding officer's desk.

"Shem, I have two soldiers who spent the night in the prison cells with bloodied faces. They say *you* gave them those bloodied faces." the commanding officer said.

"Yes sir, I did."

"And what warranted this beating that you found it necessary to rearrange their faces?"

"I found them forcing themselves on two women." The commanding officer raised his head slightly.

"I see," he said slowly, "and you thought it necessary to pummel them?" Shem's face flushed in anger and surprise at his commanding officer's comment and his composure melted.

"One was pressing up against a girl, forcibly, and the other had started unbuttoning the other girl's shirt!" he replied angrily, his voice raised.

"Watch your tone, soldier."

"Sir," Shem replied more calmly, "how can you defend them? They were caught, literally, about to rape women, and these are men of the law."

"I am not defending them, soldier. If they were conducting themselves in a manner unbecoming of the uniform they wear, then they will be reprimanded."

"Reprimanded, sir?" Shem replied back, through gritted teeth.

"Yes, reprimanded. There will be a full investigation of this incident, and upon our findings, they will be dealt with appropriately."

"Sir, with all due respect, an investigation? There shouldn't even be an investigation. They shouldn't even be allowed to put on that uniform again."

"How we decide to discipline our subordinates is *our* decision, not yours. This matter is finished; besides, you won't have to deal with them anymore. They are being transferred. Dismissed."

Shem paused a moment.

"Sir," he replied, saluted, spun on his heels and exited his commander's office.

Shem stormed down the hallway, his fury fueling his steps. His face was red with anger, his eyes flared with rage and his countenance displayed something akin to wrath. He passed by several fellow soldiers who, upon noticing him, dared not get in his way or even speak to him. Shem barely noticed anyone; his mind maddened with anger. He was infuriated that his leadership was taking this matter so lightly. He couldn't understand how they could take this matter so casually. He had to blow off steam, and so he decided to head to the sparring ring.

The sparring ring was outside near the armory, and it took Shem only a couple of minutes to reach it. He grabbed a wooden sword from the shelf of sparing weapons and pushed through the few soldiers watching the current match.

"Match is over!" he yelled. The sparring pair immediately put their weapons down and rushed to the edge of the arena when they saw Shem's determined and enraged countenance. The onlookers quickly hushed, sensing an ominous spirit about Shem.

Shem strode slowly to the center of the arena and spun around, a deep, venomous scowl on his face.

"Who wants to spar?" he yelled, the promise of death in his voice, throwing his arms in the air, and his words cutting through the air like a sword. All who heard them knew this was no ordinary sparring challenge. His words were fused with anger, with danger, with death. Those who didn't know him sensed he wasn't a man, at this moment, but an animal. None were dense enough to take him up on the offer. Those who did know him had never seen him this angry, had never seen him this enraged. Both groups of men knew not to spar with this man, turned primal from rage.

Shem slowly scanned the small crowd, dropping his hands, and his eyes fell upon two bruised faces—faces he knew well and faces that knew him too well. It was the two men he had caught forcing themselves on two women.

"You two!" he shouted, pointing his wooden sword to the two men. "Which one of you wants to spar!" The two men stood wide-eyed, no one saying a word. "What? You Cowards?" Shem taunted.

"I'll fight you," someone from the other side of the small crowd said. Shem snapped his neck toward the voice. He immediately recognized the soldier as he stepped out to grab a sparring sword. Shem knew this particular soldier; Joel, was his name. He was new and felt he had something to prove. He was arrogant and a good fighter, which fueled his arrogance. "Same rules as usual?" Joel asked as he stepped into the ring. By "rules as usual" everyone knew Joel meant no rules. Sparing matches were based on real combat, and in real combat, there were no rules. You fought until someone won.

Shem nodded. The two raised their wooden swords signaling the beginning of the match. They circled the edge of the ring like a pair of predatory creatures, each believing the other to be the prey. Shem took the first action, taking a couple of steps closer to Joel. He brought his sword up high, leaving his opposite side open, which Joel took advantage of.

Shem anticipated the attack to his open side dropped to a knee, shortening the distance he would need to bring his sword down for a block. As he dropped to his knee, he twisted his torso toward the approaching weapon, swinging his own wooden blade down into the path of Joel's sword with all his might.

Shem felt the hard jarring of the impact of the two wooden swords, though less than Joel. He knew this because of the momentum of his own sword as it continued, reversing the path of Joel's sword.

Shem took advantage of this opportunity, as Joel's

sword now forced wide by Shem's own powerful counter left Joel open for attack.

Fueled by a rage that seemed to grant him an extra measure of strength and swiftness, Shem jumped back onto both feet, bringing his wooden blade up and into the side of his opponent's calf.

Joel cried out in pain as the wood impacted, hard, on his lower leg, which sent his leg up, off the ground, as Shem continued his strike, lifting Joel's leg up as high as he could with the sword until Joel lost his balance and tumbled to the ground.

Joel quickly recovered, however, not fast enough to keep from Shem's next volley of wrath. Shem spun to face his fallen opponent who had barely managed to scramble to his feet as Shem sliced his mock sword through the air in a sideswipe to Joel's ribs. Joel managed to block some of the blow with his own mock sword, but Shem landed a heavy blow to Joel's side.

Shem advanced with no mercy, his animalistic rage overtaking him. Joel stepped farther back, bringing his sword up in a desperate attempt to defend himself from his maddened foe.

Shem swung another slice to the ribs, which Joel blocked successfully. Without hesitation, Shem recovered from the block and brought his wooden blade up into his enemy's sword again, then again, and again. With every parry, Joel became more and more desperate to flee this sparring match, which he knew now to be no sparring match, but Shem gave him no reprieve, no escape. His sword came down, and down, and down and down. Every blow made Joel weaker and weaker. Every blow caused Joel's grip on his only means of defense to loosen, just that much more.

Joel screamed for Shem to stop, but Shem couldn't hear him.

One of Shem's crazed blows contacted Joel's head,

despite his defenses, now weakened through fear, pain, and exhaustion. Then another, and another.

Joel's grip on his mock sword finally failed as another attack struck both his sword and his face. Then Shem's fist contacted between the eye socket, the nose, and the cheekbone. Joel fell to his back, eyes blurry, face warm with blood and shooting pain in his side.

The monstrous Shem before him raising his deadly stick for one final blow with a scream of furry.

Suddenly, another mock sword slammed against Shem's with a painful jarring.

"That's enough. You have won," said a deep, calm, harsh voice. Shem looked over to see Jolan, a fellow captain, and his friend. Shem looked from his friend to Joel's bloodied face as he lay on his back and an arm up to block Shem's final blow. His eyes full of fear and his face distorted with dread, the blood clinging to his face, a corporeal manifestation of his horror.

"It's over. You won," his friend said. Shem looked back to his friend who shot a quick glance at the crowd. Shem understood the meaning behind the glance and looked at the crowd. It was filled with face upon face of something akin to surprise and horror. It was only then Shem realized how far he had allowed his rage to push him. He had crossed a line, and that line could never be uncrossed. He knew anyone who saw him today would look at him differently now.

Shem lowered the wooden sword and dropped it beside Joel, then walked out of the arena, the crowd parting before him. He didn't look at anyone as they parted, now as he walked between them. He merely stared directly ahead, to the gate. His goal was anywhere but the compound.

***

Ham perused the shelves of the back stock room, marking down items he was running low on. He kept meticulous notes on his storehouse; thus, he never ran out of stock on anything, unless his orders for replenishing his items were not accomplished as expected, which happened only occasionally. After marking what he needed to order, and how many, he locked up the store, hanging a sign explaining he was on an errand and would be back in the afternoon.

It was about two hours from noonday, and the pink sun shone brightly, casting a heavy pink wash on everything. He double checked that he had his parchment in his brown leather satchel and headed for the first of his many stops. His first stop was the tanner, where he would order the various leather supplies he was low on. Next, the chandler, where he would order his candles, then the metallurgist, where he would order all his metal supplies. He had about a dozen stops to order his many supplies, including ropes, cauldrons, and herbs.

He was about halfway through his errand list and heading toward his usual herbalist's store with whom he did business when he heard the vicious growling and barking of a dog, as well as what sounded like children laughing. Then he heard the high-pitched squeal of the dog's long yelp, two more, and then one last yelp cut short, followed by gleeful shouts. Though he couldn't see what was happening, the sounds left little room for misinterpreting what was going on. Then disgusted horror filled Ham's heart as he heard another yelp, this time from what sounded like—and Ham knew to be—a pup! Ham jogged down the alley where the sounds of the yelping pup originated.

The alley soon opened up to a small field where three boys gathered around a makeshift cage, all laughing and shouting in glee. One of the boys held a large brick over his head and flung it down, hard, at his feet. The brick landed with a bone crashing thump on a small blackish blob. All the boys laughed and shouted with joy. Ham's heart sank with horror. He knew what that black blob was, and it sickened his stomach to even imagine children could do that. He leaped into a full sprint as the boys gathered around another blob, and as Ham neared he could finally make out what he already knew it to be.

The boys knelt by a puppy, each with knives, poking and cutting it. With every cut and poke, the tiny thing let out a yelp, and the boys laughed. With every yelp Ham grew nearer to the boys, his anger rising with every step. Seconds later, he was on the boys, who were too engrossed in torturing the puppy that they didn't see him charging at them until he was right on top of them. He shoved the closest to the ground and grabbed the second by the collar, lifting him to his feet and throwing him into the third boy who had scrambled to his feet started to flee. The two tumbled to the ground in a heap of entangled limbs. Ham turned to the boy whom he had shoved to see him climbing to his feet and darting off. The other two boys stumbled back to their feet and raced off as well.

Ham knelt down by the puppy and carefully looked the animal over. It appeared the wounds were not serious, though painful, he was sure. They bled as cuts and stabs do, but Ham didn't think the puppy would die from loss of blood or anything. Except its whining, the pup seemed okay. He scooped up the puppy in his hands, holding it gently and looked around for any more puppies. What he saw sunk his stomach, and if the children were still there he would probably have beat them senseless.

Inside the makeshift cage, he had noticed when he first saw the boys was a large black dog pierced to death, the three spiked sticks still protruding from the dead dog. Blood pooled around it from several more puncture wounds, and its tongue lay slack on the ground. He saw next, the block the boy had dropped, blood seeping out from under it, and he dared not pick it up. The last and most horrifying site he saw was another puppy lying in a pool of blood. Its legs had been severed from its body, and it had been left to bleed to death with its legs set up tall in a teepee.

Ham held back a stomach full of vomit and tried to think of something more pleasant. Then, the puppy started licking him. Ham had not yet realized it, but when he looked back on the moment, he knew it was the distraction he needed away from the horrifically tortured and murdered dogs.

Ham finished the rest of his errands, and when he got back to his shop, he cleared out a place in the back, setting up a small living space for the puppy. The puppy seemed to be doing a lot better in just the short time Ham had been with him. It was barking and licking, and playfully biting at him with only an occasional yelp from its injuries. When he went home, he took the puppy with him.

***

It had been two days sense Shem had "lost it" in the sparring ring, and although his troops seemed to have gotten over his tantrum in the ring, he could sense they saw him differently. He could see the fear in Joel's eyes whenever Shem neared him. He could see the trepidation in his other subordinates as well. Most of all, though, he could feel the difference in himself. His anger came more easily to him, and he had to fight harder within himself to suppress it.

The night sky cast a pink hue on the dark street, made even darker and eerier as he fell into the shadows of the towering buildings of the alleyway where he had been called. It was a long alley and turned into a connecting street in an "L" shape. He rounded the corner to the alley and what he saw didn't surprise him. He had been told it was a murder. However, he was not told that he knew this victim, nor was he told she had been raped, as well. He stopped and stood in shock for a moment as he recognized this woman, one of the very women he had saved a few nights before from being raped by soldiers. Sorrow for the young lady filled him, and he knelt, taking her cold, dead hand in his.

He looked into her lifeless, frozen eyes, ignoring the dark blood in a pool around her body and the slit across her neck. He could only imagine her fear as the man, or men (he knew who they were), forced themselves on her. He could only imagine the terror in her heart as she bled to death.

He wondered what was worse; the pain of the severing of the jugular, the choking on your own blood, the inability to breathe, or the knowledge that you were dying.

He squeezed her hand slightly.

"I am sorry this happened to you," he said. "You didn't deserve this."

His sorrow for her started morphing, then, into anger.

"You didn't deserve this," he said louder. "They will pay for what they did to you!" Without looking up from her body, he told the officer nearest him to find the two officers he had beaten when they first attempted to rape the woman.

"Uh, sir. It's late, and they are probably sleeping," the officer reported.

Rage flooded into every fiber of his being, then, like a dam releasing a river of molten lava. He lurched to his feet, spun around to the soldier, wrapped a hand around his neck, and with a strength he didn't know he had, shoved him into the brick wall.

"I don't care!" he screamed with venom. "Wake them up and get them to headquarters," he finished, grabbing him by the shoulder with both hands and shoving him into the closest soldier who stood there aghast. "Or I'll have both of your heads," he said. The two soldiers regained their composure and immediately darted around the corner.

Shem watched them leave and, without another word, headed to the compound.

Shem didn't know how long he stood at the gate waiting. There was only one thing on his mind—justice. Now there was no way his superiors could ignore this; they had to do something about the criminal actions of these so-called enforcers of the law.

When the two men he ordered to escort the two soldiers whom Shem knew had killed the girl finally arrived with their charges, Shem saw the nervousness in all of their eyes.

"Take them to the cells," Shem ordered.

Shem glared menacingly at the two officers he knew beyond a doubt had raped the woman. He let them pass by him as he stood to the side of the gate, his eyes burrowing into them. He waited a few moments and fell into step behind the four officers. He eyed the two murderous rapists up and down hatefully, noticing they had

donned their issued footwear—hard leather boots—but not

any of their other issued clothes. They both wore what

Shem assumed to be their sleeping clothes; a long-sleeved

lace-up cotton shirt and cotton trousers with a gown over

them. They, indeed, looked silly, but Shem was in no mood

for humor.

Shem followed them down to the prison cells and

waited for the two on-duty soldiers to leave. He was just

about to speak when he heard his commanding officer

shout from the entrance to the cell hallway to get to his

office. Shem looked up to see him disappear through the

door. Shem knew he was pissed from the tone in his

command and the slightly disheveled appearance.

Shem would have wondered how he knew about

this, but he also knew someone had informed the

commander of his less-than-professional behavior in the

alleyway. He glared at the two prisoners and left without

saying a word.

***

Shem entered the threshold of his home an hour after his commanding officer had called him to his office. It was late, very late. He didn't know what time it was, but he had the night shift, and though he was home early, it was still late—or early depending on how one looked at it. He closed the door behind him, then slammed a fist down on the door.

He angrily made his way to the kitchen to get some food. Immediately, he noticed Mirriam had left stew in the cauldron in the hearth, and he took the flint beside the hearth and sparked a fire to heat up his soup. He angrily poked at the fire with the poker he snatched up, becoming increasingly impatient for it to catch.

The fire finally caught, and Shem started stirring the stew with the wooden spoon Mirriam had left in the cauldron. Every so often, he would slam the spoon into the side of the cauldron, releasing a sliver of the anger boiling inside of him. He knew stirring the stew right away was pointless, but it gave him a measure of release, so after a few dozen swirls in the cauldron he let it stand and proceeded to search out and pour himself a large mug of semi-fresh orange juice his wife had squeezed that morning. Again, releasing his anger in short bursts as he periodically pounded a fist on the counter.

He bounced back and forth between stirring the stew angrily and preparing all of the materials for his meal while slamming the utensils and other items on the counter.

He hadn't realized how much noise he had been making until Mirriam groggily ambled down the steps.

"What's going on down here?" she asked.

"I'm sorry. I was just letting off some steam," he replied.

"You're home early," she acknowledged. Shem turned to stir the stew.

"Yeah, well, Commander Raizen suspended me." Shem slammed the spoon against the cauldron and spun back to face Mirriam.

"What?!" she exclaimed, more awake at the shock of the news. "Why?" She made her way down the rest of the stairs and over to Shem's side.

Shem told her of the two women he had seen about to get raped by two of his subordinates, then about finding one of them raped and murdered. He explained he had lost it and ordered two soldiers to arrest the men he stopped the other day and that because of it the commander suspended him.

He explained he lost his temper at Commander Raizen saying there wasn't a reason to hold them, or it wasn't even that big of a deal that the two men were going to rape them anyway because they were only whores.

Marriam sat down with him after that, having him sit on their couch as she prepared everything for him. She knew he needed time to process the day's events. To grieve

for this woman and to let his anger at the injustice that his

fellow law enforcers allow. She knew this wasn't the first

time Shem had come at odds with his leadership about their

lack of justice, even—as Shem would say—their

corruptness.

The two sat together saying little to each other until

Shem finally decided to go to bed.

OBSESSION

Noah raced through the night, down the many dangerous streets of Fulstron, his heart pounding and mind aflight with a thousand ideas. He didn't even notice Shem or the officers massing at the alleyway nearby. He reached his shop and quickly unlocked the door, jumped inside and darted for his drawing room. He lit several lanterns and began scribbling a sketch.

He had just been sitting at his cliff side overlooking Fulstron as he often did when a commanding voice shook him from his meditations. The voice spoke with such serene power, yet fearful uprightness, that Noah felt a flood of contradicting emotion overwhelm him. The voice told him to build a ship to save his family. That the race of man had become too evil, and man would soon be destroyed. The voice told him that he alone and his family had found grace in his sight because of their righteousness.

Noah sat a moment after the voice had given him the instructions, contemplating the monumental event that had just transpired, and what it meant for him and his family. Then, he sped off toward his workshop.

Finally, he had finished the sketches for what he knew would be the greatest accomplishment he would ever achieve—the pinnacle of his carpentry.... He knew it would take a long time…and he knew it would symbolize the end of his way of life. It was only then that he noticed the sun shining through his window. He had been up all night designing the great ship he and his family would sail into the new world! He quickly rolled his parchments and stuffed them into a small cubby hole in the corner of his drawing shop and raced home to tell his wife of the great revelation he had been shown.

***

The next morning, Noah showed up at his shop several hours before dawn, before the sun's bright rays invaded his bedroom and dragged him from his dreams, as it normally did. He simply woke. Well rested, he donned his clothes and headed off to his shop. He lit his table lanterns and worked at his shop until the sun hung brightly overhead. When the sun had risen high, Noah quit working on his projects, blew out the lanterns, snatched up the sketches for his newest project and headed into the nearby forest with his axe.

Noah cut down tree after tree, day after day until he had several dozen felled trees to begin his work. He spent most of the day working out in the forest cutting down the trees for his project, taking away from time spent on his other projects.

He only worked in his shop a few hours each day with his smaller projects, and refused work on many larger projects, even when the customers would offer to pay well above what Noah would ask. He merely told them he had a project that already took most of his time, and it wouldn't be fair to them for him to do a shoddy, rushed job on their merchandise.

After he felled the several dozen trees and removed all the limbs, he began preparations on the first step in his extensive plans. He procured several dozen cement blocks from Ham's shop to set the finished cuts on. He repeated this process over the next five months: cutting down trees, shaping the various wood pieces, and piling them on blocks. His days grew longer in the forest, and the forest inched its way smaller. His customers dwindled more and more, and his family began to become concerned. Noah had almost completely forsaken his shop and now refused any new customers, regardless of how small the job or how much they offered to pay. His income from the shop was almost nonexistent, but he offset this by bundling all the spare wood from his work and having Ham sell it in his shop or trading it for some of Ham's products. The season change was nearing, and all of Fulstron was preparing for winter weather. It would start getting cooler soon, and though the day hours wouldn't be much different, it was the nights that would become uncomfortably, but not unbearably, cold, so having a good stock of small firewood sticks to warm the house a little was a useful commodity to have. By storing up kindling, Noah had a steady income rolling in for his wife, though not as much as before. He knew, though, the One who called him to create this last masterpiece would see him through until the end.

Noah stood, now, pouring over his sketches. He had prepared enough cuts, for now, he had decided. It was time for him to start the construction of his masterpiece: his legacy that would mark the beginning of a new world. He had brought many tools he knew he would need such as a sanding block, several chisels and a hammer.

It was time for him to begin forming the keel, or in this case, three keels. His plans called for a center keel with flanking keels set twenty feet from the center keel, each eight feet thick. He found the felled trees he had set aside for the keels with a diameter big enough to cut and sand into eight-foot-thick beams, fastened them to harnesses with oxen secured to the opposite ends, and guided the powerful beasts to where he wanted his beams laid.

***

Noah finally finished shaping the beams. He spent day after day cutting and chiseling the trees into beams of the desired size. A few days later, he finished cutting the end notches and making his wooden dowels to fasten them together. His last steps were to secure each of the enormously long beams into their counterpart notches, drill the dowel holes and secure the dowels in their respective holes with tree sap, essentially cementing them together.

With the help of his oxen, he secured the beams together and began his drilling. It was a tedious job, but it was relatively easy, as his drilling tool was very easy to handle, a corkscrew device with a jagged tip—simple to

82

use, yet effective and efficient. The hand drill was shaped in a blocky "S" configuration with a jagged edge at its point and two handles, one in the center of the "S" and the other at the top. He merely held it secure with one hand on the center handle and twisted the corkscrew drill around with the other hand.

After the drilling, all he needed to do was pour some tree sap in the holes and drop the dowels in and he would be done with the first step of his masterpiece.

A GROWING FAITH

Ham strolled up to his father who stood at the edge of a large forest sanding down the finishing touches of a board. It had been half a year since his father had begun this obsession with whatever it was he was working on. Noah had closed his shop and had begun focusing all his spare time on this project. Early mornings and late evenings he would work, before dawn and well into the night. He pulled his coat tight. It was the beginning of winter now, and it was beginning to get uncomfortable in the evenings.

Ham was amazed at how much his father had accomplished in such little time. He noticed as he neared that several dozen of the surrounding trees had been cut down to only just a few feet off the ground. Several yards off to Noah's side lay a large pile of dead or dying branches and wood scraps. Just a few feet to his other side lay neatly stacked piles of wooden beams and planks, too many to count.

Noah finished sanding and saw his son as he looked up from his work.

"Ah!" he said, "Perfect timing. Help me with this," he said and waved to the end of the board. Ham obediently grabbed the opposite end. "On three…one…two…three." The two hefted the board to a nearby pile, then caught their breath.

"What brings you out here?"

"Just came by to see what you have been working on. You're never at your shop anymore," Ham replied as he followed his father to a cut portion of a fallen tree. Again, Ham obediently hefted the heavy tree, and the two carried it to the woodworking stands Noah had set up when he first began his project.

"You just wanted to see me, is that it?" Noah replied. Ham could tell from his tone his father knew he wasn't there to just check up on him. Ham smiled.

"Mom's worried about you," he said. "We are all worried about you. What are you making out here all day, every day?" Noah smiled.

"Well, I'm almost done, I think, with the first steps of my plans, so I'll show you." Noah led him to a small bench, which held his sketches secured by a rock.

"Look, son." Ham scanned the sketches, flipping slowly through the pages.

"A boat!" he exclaimed, exasperated. "You're building a giant boat? There's no water for miles."

"There will be when I'm done."

Ham looked up at his father. "What are you going to do when people start realizing what it is you're building? They're going to say you're crazy!"

Noah turned. "Let them," he said and returned to carving away at the log.

"Dad, why are you building a boat on dry land? What is it you think this will accomplish?" Noah stopped carving and looked up at his son.

"I'm going to save the world," he said flatly. Ham stared in shock. He didn't know what to say. "The world is going to end when I finish this ship, and only those on it will be saved. The world is going to be flooded, and the ship is our salvation," he explained.

"What are you talking about?" Ham asked. Noah stopped his work again and told him of his encounter on the cliffside, and the voice that told him to build the boat. That the world was going to be flooded and the boat would save anyone who would enter it. He told Ham how they would save the animals in the boat as well.

Again, Ham didn't know what to say.

"You truly believe this?" he asked at last.

Noah nodded.

"And I can't persuade you otherwise?" Noah shook his head.

Ham nodded. "Well. I'll talk to you later, Dad." Noah nodded and watched his son leave.

Things were changing now. Ham was a sign of that, but he couldn't stop now. The fate of the world depended on him. His family depended on him, even if they didn't realize it yet.

***

Noah and Naomi sat at the dinner table eating vegetable stew and bread. Naomi sat unusually silent, a look of concern on her face as she stared at Noah's bandaged shoulder. He had come home early with a gaping cut in the back of his shoulder, and she had stitched and dressed it. It was a bad cut, and painful, she knew, but Noah kept on with his business as if nothing had happened; the only indication that his injury bothered him was an occasional grimace when he stretched his arm too far. He had cut himself from the shoulder down diagonally to almost the middle of his back. He insisted it looked worse than it was, which she didn't believe. When she asked what had happened, he said he had been hoisting a large beam up with a pulley and the pulley broke, catching him on the way down.

They had had many conversations about his project. Ham had told her two weeks earlier that he was building a boat, and she had pressed further into his reasoning for such a bizarre project so far from any water. He had told her God had spoken to him and told him the world was going to end, that he was going to send a flood, and Noah was to build a boat to preserve animal and mankind. She knew when he had told her this—she could see it in his eyes, hear it in his voice, feel his passion for it—that he believed what he was saying to the core of his being, and there was no dissuading him from his course. She had never been concerned for his safety, though, and as she stared at the bandage, she grew increasingly concerned.

"What if it happens again?" she asked. Noah looked up from his soup.

"What?" he replied.

"What if you get injured again? Something more serious and no one is there to help you?"

"It won't. I'll be safer. I'll pay more attention," he replied, trying to appease her.

"You're always careful, Noah," she replied with a tinge of anger. "I don't like you working out there all by yourself." Noah smiled.

"It's no different from working in the shop all by myself," he replied. "And you have never had a problem with me working in my shop by myself."

"You have never come home with such a bad injury." Noah smiled again.

"Well if you're so worried about me working out there by myself then you could come help."

"I am serious, Noah!" she retorted.

"You're right. I'm sorry for making light of your concerns. We will just have to have faith that the One who called me will see me through until the end," he replied. Naomi looked at Noah a few more seconds and resigned herself to keeping faith that Noah wouldn't be seriously injured during this project and went back to finishing her stew.

A few minutes later, Noah finished his stew and cleared his dishes from the table.

"Have faith, my love," he whispered in her ear and kissed her cheek. "I love you," he added as he straightened back up and headed off to bed.

Naomi sat staring into her stew.

"With all the wickedness," she whispered, "in the world, you brought me the one shining light." Her eyes drifted up as she continued. "If you are going to destroy everything, and if you did tell him to build that boat, and you will see him through it, then help me. Help me not to worry. Help me not to fear. Help me not to doubt." She stood, snatching up her dishes and cleared the table, then headed to bed herself, her heart heavy with concern for her husband.

***

Noah guided his oxen and wagon up to Ham's shop. The wagon was a simple design, easily built for anyone who had even a shred of carpentry skill. A simple harness connected the oxen to the wagon. The wagon itself was a skeleton frame, lacking any bottom or side planking, its contents were bundles of wood. Noah snatched up a bundle and opened the heavy wooden door to Ham's shop. Using one of the sticks from the bundle as a doorstop, he jammed it under the door. Satisfied the door would stay open, he grabbed a second bundle and headed into Ham's shop. He dropped the bundles with a few others that were already placed near the door and piled several more bundles with them. For the rest of the bundles, he maneuvered his way through the shop and into the back where he stacked them in overstock with Ham, who had been straightening his shelves when Noah entered and started helping him.

"Hey Dad, let me help with that," Ham said as he noticed Noah stacking up the bundles by the door. Noah handed Ham the bundles and snatched a couple more from his wagon while Ham stacked them as neatly as they would stack.

"Hold on," Ham ordered after about half a dozen bundles. "Let me grab a couple bundles and we'll start taking them to the back." He snatched up two bundles and the two headed to the back of the store.

"I was wondering when you were going to bring these by. I was starting to get low, as you saw." Ham said.

"Well, I wanted to finish working on the stern of the boat before making a trip to town," Noah replied.

"How is that coming along?" Ham asked as they dropped the bundles in a pile and headed back to get several more loads.

"Long hours, but I think it's coming along nicely," Noah replied.

"Nicely, huh? How is that cut?" Ham said with a smirk.

"Your mom told you, did she."

"Yeah. She's a bit worried about you, that you will get hurt.

"She's overreacting."

"Maybe, but I think this whole thing you're doing is silly. I mean—a boat out in the middle of the dry land hundreds of miles away from the ocean. Kinda' crazy, dad."

"Ah, so you think I'm crazy," Noah jested.

"I didn't say that."

Noah patted him on the shoulder. "I know son. I may be crazy after all, but I can't deny what I heard." They both snatched up three more bundles, tucking one under an arm.

"Yeah, the voice of God telling you the world is going to end and that it's your job to save it—by building a boat."

"Exactly!"

"Well, Dad, forgive me if I find that hard to believe. I mean, you instilled in us knowledge of some kind of higher power—of God—and that we should try to please God by being honest and kind, by not being evil." They dropped their bundles, and again, returned for more. "But God destroying the world and telling you that you will be the savior of anyone who will listen—I mean, sounds a bit far-fetched don't you think?" Noah simply smiled.

"Indeed, it does. Indeed it does, but isn't that what faith is all about? Believing in something we can't prove?

Or even believing in something you have no reason, sometimes, to believe in?"

Snatching up several more bundles and returning to the shop, they continued their conversation.

"I guess, Dad. One thing is for sure: you sure do have a lot more faith than I do."

"For now, my son, for now," Noah replied, gently nudging him with a shoulder.

"Well, anyway, I told Mom I would check on you and help you after I close my shop every day. Just to make sure you're okay, and you don't hurt yourself again."

"Well, I could use the company and the help. It will make the day go by quicker, I think." They dropped the bundles in the pile and continued bringing the rest in, talking more about everyday life, and how their families were doing. When the wagon was empty, they said their farewells and returned to their daily routines.

***

Ham and Noah stood over the plans for Noah's ark. Noah was explaining his process for making the ribs of the boat. They had been working a week on sizing and cutting the felled trees for the first rib beams.

He was explaining they would need to make a device to bend the wood designated for the curved bottom of the boat, which Noah had already designed as well. They would have to make that first, so they could tie one end of the beam to a rope, Noah had explained. The rope would be run through a large beam for support to which oxen would pull the other end of the rope until the water-soaked rib curved to their desired position. Once the beam was set, they would secure the rope with a notched wheel device that would wind up the excess rope. Once the rope was at the desired tension, they would keep it secure by locking the wheel into the corresponding notch.

Noah explained they would make at least half a dozen so they could do several ribs at the same time. After building the device, they would cut the ribs and begin forming the ones they wanted curved, letting them dry while they sized, cut and placed the others. He explained the beams would need to be notched and cut, cemented together with dowels and pitch and that he expected to lay several straight ones together on the bottom with the curved ones for the curve of the ship and several more straight ones up the sides.

They worked on the bending device for several days, and to Ham's amazement, they had finished making the entire thing in less than a week. It was massive. It had half a dozen support beams and stood a good ten to fifteen feet high. The beams themselves were the thickness of a man. Along the ground lay a grounding beam the length of the device, which had another half dozen beams set along the ground connected to another grounding beam. The four ground corners of the massive bending device were tied to felled tree trunks to hold it in place while the top two beams were tied to unfelled trees Noah had purposed for the task before he had even begun cutting down trees.

It surprised Ham, as well, that Noah hadn't needed to replace or sharpen any of his cutting or drilling tools since Ham had been working with him, and they seemed just as sharp as when he had started.

Now that they had finished making the device, they would begin making the ribs of the boat, starting with the ones to be bent. Noah had explained to Ham that when the beams were cut and shaped they would take them to the nearby lake about half a mile away and let them sit overnight soaking up the water, and the next day, they would bend them.

They were long days for Ham as he helped his father, but they were even longer days for Noah, though Noah, by this time, had gotten used to the long days. Noah worked fast during the day and even quicker when his son was helping, and they accomplished more than they thought possible. When they finished the first batch of ribs Ham guided several oxen with the first of the ribs to be bent to the nearby lake and deposited the beams for their overnight stay into the water.

When Ham reached the lake, he immediately noticed the loading point his father had explained to him. There was a large ramp for the oxen to walk up and beneath the ramp, under the surface of the water, was another frame to catch the rib beams. Ham could tell the frame was low enough to ensure the beams stayed submerged—Ham wondered how his father could have secured this frame and ramp all by himself.

He led each ox onto the ramp, ensuring the ribs slid into the slots between the ramp sections and submerged into the water, then secured the beams to the frame.

The next day, as it had become regular as clockwork, early evening Ham strode up to Noah's work area. To his surprise, he saw Noah and Naomi sitting on a blanket eating bread. Noah was pointing to the different piles of wood. Ham knew he was explaining his plans, which was confirmed when his father jumped up and dragged Naomi over to the blueprints.

They finally noticed Ham as he was almost on top of them.

"Ham, look who's joining us!" his father exclaimed as he motioned toward Naomi.

"I see that," Ham replied with a smile. "hi, Mom." She smiled and hugged him in reply.

"Well, I'm going to get back to work," Noah reported excitedly.

Ham and Naomi watched him as he quickly fell into his work routine with a rejuvenated bolster.

"Mom, what are you doing here? I thought you didn't want Dad working on this silly project.

Naomi sat back down on the blanket; Ham followed suit.

"Remember our conversation about my concern for Noah after he came with that big cut?"

"Yeah, you asked me to start coming out to check on him."

"Well, the night that he got hurt I asked for faith to believe. Since then, I have felt better and better about him working out here, and a few days ago, I had this dream of black clouds covering everything, and we were all on this boat in the middle of the ocean. I don't know if it really means anything, but I think it might mean what Noah was told is true." Ham nodded.

"I see," he replied, unsure of how to respond. It did sound a little unusual to believe based almost solely on a dream, but he supposed if God really did call his father to do this, then if he wanted to, he could impart that same faith through a dream—he guessed.

"Well, I'm going to get to work, helping Dad."

"Okay"

Ham, soon fell into the work routine, noticing the ribs he had taken to the lake were resting in the bender as Noah had started calling it.

Naomi sat watching the two work until the day's end and they all left for their homes.

His mother was there the next day as well and the day after that, and the next, until it became expected. Gradually, Noah had given her more and more complex tasks to do as she showed her skill with woodworking. At first, he just had her sanding down the woodcuts into smooth beams, then had her drill the holes needed, and now she was even working alongside the two of them shaping and cutting the wood.

Ham had to admit, he enjoyed working alongside his parents, and before he knew it, he was putting in half days at his shop and spending the rest working on the boat. He even had to admit, as he thought about his parents and his mom's conversion, that he was starting to believe, himself. He didn't know if it was just the fact that he stayed working all day, working alongside his parents, or what. He supposed he was starting to believe. Why else would he be closing shop early and losing money? He wasn't sure if he believed fully, but he started wondering if there might be something to this calling his parents felt.

***

Shem stood in the corner of the Red Fist Tavern scrutinizing the patrons. It had been over six months since Shem had first been suspended from duty. It wasn't long after that the "investigation" as they called it, resulted in the loss of his job. As a result, he had to search out a new means to support his wife, which landed him in the Red Fist Tavern. It was notorious for having the most disorderly and wildly ruthless patrons in all of Fulstron.

Across the room stood another sentinel charged with keeping the peace—as well as it could be kept in a place like this. It was their job to quell any fights before they got out of hand.

They both wore black from head to toe; a uniform, of sorts, indicating they were not to be trifled with.

He and his counterpart had to break up at least half a dozen fights daily, some ending with almost a full-out brawl, and most included a weapon of some kind hidden away in the folds of a shirt or pant leg or coat. Every night, Shem would return home with a bruise or worse somewhere from a lucky hit. Tonight, was no different. It was nearing the end of his shift, and he noticed a group of men sitting at a table begin to get violent toward another table of patrons.

A long-bearded stout man had slammed his chair into the table behind him as he stood, at which the two men behind him took offense. The two rose to their feet angrily cursing and shouting at the robust drunken man, to which his counterpart jumped up yelling threats at the two.

Shem and his fellow sentinel promptly maneuvered themselves to flank the four men; Shem nearest the two lanky men that instigated the confrontation and Lumus nearest the robust, bearded man and his friend.

"I suggest you all sit down before you make some decisions you will regret," Lumus said.

It seemed on cue the four redirected their anger to the two of them. Lightning fast, and without hesitation, Shem brought out from his trouser pocket a short, thin wooden cudgel. The cudgel was about one and a half feet long and an inch and a half in diameter with a handle adding a few more inches to its length.

The first of Shem's targets didn't even see the cudgel and was gasping for air on his back with a bloodied face before he even knew what had happened.

The second bar patron took advantage of the few seconds Shem took to down his first opponent, and unsheathed a dagger from his hip, striking at Shem.

Shem easily dodged the slow drunkard and brought his cudgel into the man's forearm. Shem then dropped the man with a powerful fist to the temple.

Shem glanced in Lumus' direction to see Lumus

standing over the other two men.

"He told you," Shem mocked as he picked up the first of his foes and dragged the man to the entrance tossing him out the door. Behind him, Lumus drug the first of his two attackers, and both treated their second attackers in like manner, then returned to their respective corners as if nothing happened.

The bar patrons returned to their own conversations after a comment or two about the fight. Shem overheard a pair at the bar only a few feet away discussing Shem's tactics. Shem didn't recognize the pair and so knew they were not regulars. He heard one of the two mention the Legionnaire Corps, which piqued his interest, so he started eavesdropping.

The conversation turned from discussing the tactics Shem used and how it looked very similar to the Legionnaire training combat techniques, to Shem himself.

The barkeep—overhearing the conversation as

well—leaned over to mention Shem had been in the Legionnaire Corps before landing his current job.

The two glanced his way, Shem pretended not to notice as he scrutinized the rest of the patrons. The conversation began to turn, then, to the rumors that had been floating through Fulstron about a soldier in the Legionnaire Corps who went crazy. How the soldier's father went crazy at the same time. They talked about the crazy old man making a boat on the hill.

Throughout the entire conversation, the two glanced periodically toward Shem and darted their eyes away whenever Shem glanced their way or downed another mug of ale to hide their glances when he saw them.

Of course, Shem made it a point to focus his peripheral vision on the two as he glanced around the room. Soon enough, as the two drew back more and more mugs of ale, Shem didn't have to eavesdrop, as they grew louder and louder.

"Pshhh. That crazy old man. Somebody should put that lunatic out of his misery," said one.

"His crazy son, too!" the other exclaimed as he patted his friend on the shoulder.

They laughed.

"I'll bet that old man talks to animals, too, out there," the first added.

"Hey, I'll bet this guy is the son!" the second yelled. "Crazy soldier, I'll cut him down, him and his whole crazy family!" He spun around to face Shem, who, at this point, was no longer hiding the fact that he was listening.

"Hey, you," the man said. "You're the son of that crazy old man building that boat, aren't you?"

Shem ignored him.

"Hey, I'm talking to you. I see you lookin' right at me." Shem continued to ignore him, staring right at him.

"Look, Rufus, he is the crazy soldier. He's looking right at me, but nothin's getting through." He smacked

112

Rufus on the shoulder as he stood up. Rufus laughed through a mug of ale as the man took a few steps toward Shem.

"Hey you, crazy, why don't you go up to that hill with your crazy old man and talk to those animals and ghosts and flowers. Ha ha ha ha." The man pulled back for a punch and suddenly was on a table, Shem's hand around his neck and the other grabbing his wrist.

"You will stay down if you know what's good for you," he said and released the man.

Rufus sat there in shock a moment, then erupted in a loud, boisterous laugh. The other man clumsily removed himself from the table, glaring at Shem as he returned to his stool.

The rest of the night, Shem eyed the two menacingly as often as he could, his mind drifting back to the remnants of the conversation.

His father was indeed eccentric, Shem thought, but

if he were crazy, at least he wasn't doing any harm. Shem hadn't even talked to his father about his obsession with building that boat. In fact, since getting fired, his relationships with all his family had not been what they used to be. He rarely saw them now that he worked in the Red Fist Tavern. The only one he really felt close to these days was his wife, but even their relationship felt more strained than usual. He would need to fix that.

***

Ham and Dinah sat at the dinner table, an oil lantern burning and the fireplace blazing, casting a gentle glow throughout the living room and kitchen. Like many homes, it was really just one large room separated only by a counter that identified the back of the room as the kitchen and dining area. It had been a month and a half that he had been helping his father with the ark.

He sat eating a plateful of vegetables, as he discussed the day's events with his wife. First, he talked about the events at the store and then the events at the building site of the ark.

"I want to go with you tomorrow," Dinah said rather abruptly.

"Really?" Ham asked, a little surprised.

"Yeah. I don't do anything real important here, at least nothing I can't do some other day. I want to go see what's got you closing the store early and out all day away from me, and what has your mother spending all day up there too." Ham nodded, and the two finished their meal, Ham talking about building the ark and the integral process and blueprints Noah had set up. Dinah simply listened.

***

The next day, Ham closed the store just after noonday, the sun shining brightly overhead in the bright pink sky. He met his wife at home, and the two ventured to the building site of the ark.

Noah and Naomi both raised a hand in greeting as they saw the two nearing. Ham and Dinah waved back.

"Hi," Naomi said when Ham and Dinah had finally reached them, as she stood to give Dinah a hug. "What are you doing out here?" she asked joyously. Dinah looked at Ham, then back to Naomi

"I just wanted to see what's been keeping my husband away from me," she replied facetiously as she sat down.

"Ah, that would be my fault," Noah replied.

Dinah's eyes floated to the grand sight before her of the massive wooden devices that assisted in the creation of the ark, and the various woodcuts and the skeletal beginnings of the ark.

Noah noticed her attention on what would be his greatest of achievements and immediately started to explain her surroundings to her, his passion evident. He soon suggested he show her his blueprints, and Naomi countered the suggestion by telling Noah to let them eat, seeing Dinah had not yet begun removing their food from her basket she had brought with her. Noah apologized and allowed his son and daughter-in-law to eat.

After they had all eaten, Noah showed Dinah his blueprints. She had to admit; she was intrigued, now, having seen everything that was going on and looking over the blueprints. Noah had thought of everything. He had places to warm water, devices to make non-drinkable water drinkable, storage for food and extra wood, and even a section to grow fruits and vegetables.

"Noah," she asked, after looking over the blueprints. "I don't see a list of supplies we will need when we're in the ark. Where's your list of supplies?"

"Supplies?" he asked dumbfoundedly.

"You know, bedding, clothing, tables, cookware."

"Oh," he replied. "I haven't really thought about all of that stuff yet."

"I see. Well, don't you think we should start at least figuring out what we need to take?"

"Umm…sure. Go ahead."

"What? You want me to do it?"

"Well, yeah. After all, *you* brought it up, didn't you?"

"I guess, but…well…okay. I guess I can make a list."

She couldn't explain it, but she was excited to start making the list. She wasn't even sure she believed this end-of-the-world stuff. She did trust Noah and did believe in the God Noah worshiped. She trusted in Noah's God…in Ham's God. But if Noah's God, her God, did tell Noah to build this ark and save his family then it would happen, and she had better get on board.

She found a piece of parchment, an ink bottle and a quill to her surprise. She realized, then, after finding all she needed, that it looked as if Noah's entire shop was out there. Crates and boxes of random tools and items…like the ink and quill. She chuckled to herself and started writing.

***

Japheth sat in a skiff amidst a vast sea. The rain fell in large, fast, hard, cold drops that stung as they exploded on his skin. It fell in sheets and froze him to the bone. It clung to his clothes like death. It rained with a fury he couldn't have ever imagined. He had never seen rain, and as it flooded the boat, utter fear washed over him just as the rain washed over the world.

On the other side of the skiff sat his wife, drenched in rain, her clothes sticking to her, weighed down with the heaviness of the water-soaked material. The two looked at each other with despair, knowing they had both made the wrong choice.

Surrounding them in this new vast sea being pelted by the thick, hard, rain was drifting debris and bodies scattered as far as they could see. Wood from what once were homes, carriages, toys once used by children, and much, much more floated idly by as the two sat, hopelessly waiting for the inevitable.

Men, women, children, dogs, cats, rats and other creatures bobbed in the new sea's currents. The couple refused to look at the lifeless bodies and just stared at each other.

The skiff was quickly filling with water, but the couple did nothing to prevent it. They had been frantically trying to scoop up the water filling the boat, but quickly realized it was a futile effort.

Noah, Shem, Ham, Naomi, Dinah and Mirriam all stood on the deck of their boat, safe and secure. They stared out at Japheth and Zaphira as the ship passed by.

Japheth and Zaphira stared back as they noticed the massive ship and the family passing by only yards away, yet so unreachable.

The current pulled the family farther, and farther

away, all the while the downpour of rain filling the skiff more and more.

They heard a sound, then, as the ark floated safely in the distance. It was a faint roar that seemed to grow steadily louder and louder. Terror filled the couple as they saw the source of that sound. A rush of water, heading straight for them, larger than anything they have ever even imagined. It churned and bubbled as it closed, like a frothy white beastly muzzle baring down on them, anticipating its next meal. The sound became deafening as the surge of water grew near. Zaphira and Japheth squeezed each other close in horror, knowing they were about to die.

The water plowed into them drowning what was left of the skiff above the water and sending the two into the unrelenting depths of the ocean, the force tearing them away from each other.

Japheth saw his wife drifting away surrounded in a cloud of bubbles as the churning water disrupted itself, and

Zaphira let out the last breath she would ever breathe. He felt his own air leave him and saw the bubbles surrounding him. He heard something, then, that jarred him to the core of his being. He heard it clear as day, clear as if he were standing in the open, clear as if he were standing on dry land.

"This will be you if you don't go with your family."

Suddenly, he woke.

Japheth and Zaphira both awoke, their breaths heavy and sheets damp with sweat. They both sat up in silence, dropping their feet off the edge of the bed, their backs turned toward each other, the pink hue of the night moonlight seeping in slivers through the bedroom curtains adding to their uneasiness.

"Did you have a nightmare too?" Zaphira asked at length.

"Yes. We drowned," Japheth replied.

"While everybody else was on Noah's boat?"

122

"Yeah."

"What happened in the water?"

"A voice said it would happen if we didn't get on the boat."

"Japheth," Zaphira said, her voice tinged with fear. "Was it real?"

Japheth turned around.

"I think," he replied softly, "it will be real if we don't get on Dad's boat."

"Me too. It was so scary. I don't want ANY of it to happen."

"I know. Me neither, but I think it WILL happen no matter what, but we can at least be safe."

"What should we do?" Japheth thought a moment.

"We should start helping." Zaphira nodded and the two laid back in bed, their heads reeling with emotions and thoughts neither wanted to voice aloud. Eventually, the two drifted back off to sleep to wake up the next morning with an unusual peace and joy despite their shared nightmare they both now believed to be a warning from God.

Japheth and his wife strode up to Noah's massive half-finished skeletal ark. It was their first time out to see the boat and Noah's new workshop, and they were truly amazed at the site. Before them stood the biggest boat, they had ever seen or even heard of. The skeletal frame itself looked like the bones of a giant beast. Several levels of bamboo scaffolding surrounded the massive ship where the ribs had been placed, Japheth counted three levels in total. The ship and scaffolding were truly a magnificent sight to see. Piles and piles of different sizes of cut wood lay near the ark and a handful of oxen grazing a few yards off in a large fenced off area. A large device tied to trees with massive wood beams tied off to the side near the oxen cage.

Ham, Naomi and Noah worked at the far end of the ark, securing a massive rib to the notched end of one of the curved ribs of the ark, making one massively long rib.

Noah and Ham stood on the scaffolding while Naomi slowly guided a couple of oxen that lifted the massive rib up through a set of pulley systems, and Dinah sat at a desk pouring over parchments.

The two couldn't help but chuckle at the sight of their father's desk sitting out there in the wilderness and Dinah working as if she were working inside an office.

Japheth and Zaphira took in the sight a few more moments. Then Japheth began his way up the scaffolding ramps as Zaphira walked over to Dinah. They offered their services, and the family quickly integrated them into the work process. Japheth helped to build the ark, and Zaphira was tasked with assisting Dinah.

The morning went smoothly, and before Japheth and Zaphira knew it, it was lunchtime. With Japheth helping to cut and place the rib sections, work went by even more quickly. Japheth, like his brother when he first started helping his father, was astonished at how quickly the work was getting done. He soon noticed, as well, the tools never dulled.

The six sat down on a blanket Naomi had prepared for the meal time, as she did every day. The family hadn't been expecting Japheth and Zaphira so they each shared a portion of their own meals prepared beforehand.

"So, Japheth, Zaphira, what brings you out here today?" Noah asked. The two glanced at each other.

"We had a dream," Japheth replied.

"What do you mean you had a dream?" Ham asked. Japheth recounted their dream, explaining they both had had the same dream.

"I would have said a year ago that that was unbelievable, but now I don't put anything past our God," Ham replied. The family agreed.

"We decided if we needed to be on this boat then we better help," Japheth added. "After all, my store is all but closed. Nobody really comes anymore to buy anything, so I figured why not just start closing early and start helping out here."

"And I sit around the house all day now and try not to go to the city anymore," Zaphira interjected.

Naomi and Dinah didn't need an explanation as to why she didn't venture into the city anymore. They both felt the same way; they were treated as outcasts, diseased things. Nobody wanted to do business with them and almost always overcharged them

"Ah, sorry about that," Noah replied. "It's the crazy old guy's fault." The family all smiled at the remark.

The family relaxed a while talking more about the boat, life, everything and anything; then they got back to work.

***

Ham neared his shop yet again to find its outer walls defaced. This time, however, as he got closer, he noticed someone had shattered the window as well. He sighed in resignation, used to this by now. He had gotten the window replaced just weeks ago.

Over the last several months, his shop had increasingly become the target of vandalization. It started out as a simple collection of slurs toward him and his family, particularly his father. After a while, it grew to the defacing of a few little trinkets he kept outside, then it had escalated to threats and finally breaking the window.

It wasn't difficult to have a window replaced, only expensive. Ham didn't know the process of creating the windows, but from what he did understand, it was a long and arduous process to make a transparent window. As a result, it always took a long time and was very pricey. Now, he had to order a new window yet again.

Last time, the vandals only smashed it, leaving large cracks, but this time they shattered the window entirely.

As he came to his shop and peered inside, he noticed even more vandalization. He had gotten used to blood smears on his windows, and the walls on the outside, but now it progressed to inside his shop. He stepped through the missing window in frustration and glanced around his shop.

On several walls, blood had been smeared in degrading messages, and throughout the store, it looked as if the blood had been randomly thrown onto shelves and items.

At first, he had reported the vandalizing to the Legionnaire Corps, but they hadn't seemed to be concerning themselves with it. Ham didn't know if it was because they knew he was Shem's brother, or that he was Noah's son—or both. He quickly gave up on any help from the Corps.

Ham pulled out his cleaning supplies and started cleaning what he could of the blood from the walls and shelves. He knew there would be many unsalvageable items, but maybe, he thought, he could give them to his dad. He might make use of them.

He boarded up the window and spent the next several hours cleaning without interruption. He mulled over the idea of closing his store permanently. He didn't get many customers these days, and he had really started to enjoy working with his father out in the open.

Over the past several months Japheth's shop was vandalized in the same manner as Ham's. The final straw for Japheth, like Ham, was when his store was broken into and blood thrown onto the racks of clothes. Japheth had decided that day he would close shop and transport all of the clothing to his father's project on the hill. Ham had been closing his shop early anyway to go to help his father. As he worked, the more frustrated he became, and the more he considered closing his shop and helping his father full time.

***

Noah, Japheth, and Ham worked day in and day out shaping the ribs, then fastening them to the ark, and "cementing" them together with pitch, and then starting the process all over again.

Dinah and Zaphira worked on preparing the supplies for their journey. Zaphira looked over all of the work Dinah started and added anything she thought Dinah had left off. They checked, double checked, and triple checked to make sure they hadn't forgotten anything. They had a list of food and supplies needed: clothing, bedding, spare wood for heat, utensils, salves, scents, and anything else they could think of for any conceivable need that might arise. They calculated how much of each item they would need, especially food, and added extra, just to be safe. They concentrated on necessities first, then added comforts. They focused on the most efficient use of space. They took their time and soon recruited Mirriam for a fresh pair of eyes.

She, too, soon became as enthralled as everyone else in helping.

The family had already relocated all of Japheth's and Ham's items from their shops near the ark, so when Zaphira, Mirriam and Dinah had officially finalized their list, they began stockpiling the non-perishable items such as pots, pans, tubs and the like next to the boat in its own separate pile to start moving them into the ark when it was finished. When that task was done, they helped to build the ark until the time came to begin securing the perishable items.

***

Zaphira had been working with the family for two weeks at this point when they recruited Marriam. She, too, had noticed the city shunning her, so she ventured into the city as little as possible. Mirriam had heard one day when she went to the market that her whole family—except Shem and her, of course, had all started to help "the crazy old man," so she decided she would visit and see this boat that had Noah's entire family crazed. That decision landed her alongside her "crazed" family. At first, it was just something to occupy her time when she had nothing else to do. However, she soon found herself spending more and more time helping with the boat, and she enjoyed it. She didn't *really* believe in what Noah had been preaching to them when he saw them, but it was interesting, at the least. By the middle of her third week, they had finished hauling their stockpile and started working on the boat with the others. It seemed God was, indeed, with them, for all three women had shown extraordinary understanding and skill in carpentry and hardly even needed lessons. Again, once they showed their competence in the tasks they had been assigned, Noah gave them more demanding jobs, and when they excelled at those, he gave them even more advanced tasks until they all were working alongside Noah and the others.

ARRIVAL

The rest of the family saw Shem racing toward them on his horse at full gallop as he rounded the crest of a small hill. One by one, they saw him, and one by one, they stopped working. They knew something was wrong. Shem had never been there, and now, he raced toward them. They set their tools down and stepped out to meet him as he neared. He didn't slow until he was almost on top of them. They all saw excitement, wonder and fear in his eyes.

"It's true!" he said and stepped down off his horse. "It's all true, everything you said!"

"What are you talking about, son?" Noah asked.

"Everything you have been telling me. It's true. You were right! They're here!"

"Shem," Ham exclaimed. "You're not making any sense. Slow down." Shem took a moment to catch his breath and slow his thoughts.

"Animals—animals of all kinds coming this way. They just came through town. People started attacking them, elephants, lions, wolves, even bears. They didn't have a chance," he explained more calmly.

"They killed all the animals?" Japheth asked.

Shem shook his head.

"No, the animals killed everyone. It was a slaughter."

"They killed everybody?" Noah asked.

"No, they walked right past me, barely even noticing me. A bear even looked at me while it walked past. At first, I thought I was dead, but it just walked on by. My heart was beating out of my chest. I think they only attacked those who were a danger to them. They passed by a lot of people without even acknowledging them.

"So, it begins," Noah said. "Come, let's get you water," he suggested.

"Dad!" Ham shouted. "Look." He pointed to the hill rise Shem had passed just a few moments before. Everyone immediately lifted their gaze to the hilltop. There, a single lion stood, alone, it's tail and head held high. It turned its head upward in a long, loud, great roar.

The family stood silent, watching the terrifying beast in amazement. The roar subsided, and beasts of all kinds appeared over the crest of the hill as the lion strode down the hilltop. The most recognizable were the bears, elephants, and rhinoceros—the largest of the animals. It was a truly awe-inspiring sight, and the family all stood watching as more and more of the beasts rounded the hilltop.

Soon, the entire plain, devoid of the trees that once populated it, was now filled with scores of animals. It took a long while before any of the family moved, and it was only after the great lion, the largest of his pride, padded over to Noah in all its magnificence, stopping mere inches from him. It stood on its hind haunches, leaned its heavy paws on Noah's shoulders, and with a whine, gave Noah a sloppy wet lick with its massive tongue.

Noah's heart beat faster every second the lion neared, and he could swear he almost had a heart attack as the lion reared up and rested its paws on him. Then, his heart rate tripled as the lion scraped its sand-paper like tongue across his face, inhaling in fearful exhilaration.

The lion hopped off Noah and padded back to its pride. The family stood there in utter shock, unsure how to react. A chuckle finally broke the awkward silence, and the rest of the family added their own laughs as Noah finally wiped the slobber from his face and laughed himself.

"That was utterly amazing," Japheth exclaimed, "how it just walked up and licked you."

"Scared me to death is what it did. I think I may need new leggings," Noah replied.

They, of course, didn't get much work done the rest of the day. If they started a project, they were soon distracted by the goings-on of the animals. Mostly, though, they were distracted by the sight of all the magnificent creatures that roamed before them. The animals segregated themselves into groupings, claiming appropriate sizes of land. The lions pride claimed the shade near the ark between a pack of wolves and a sleuth of bears, and a band of gorillas claimed a section of land in the shade near the sleuth of bears. Among the animals claiming space on the opposite side of the ark were a crash of rhino's, a herd of elephants and a drove of oxen.

Off near the tree line of the forest, a tower of giraffes claimed their portion of land, and between the giraffes and ark, sheep, horses, goats, buffalo, and cows all claimed land segments of their own. A troop of kangaroos kept close to the ark near a litter of pigs. Near the pigs, a nest of rabbits of all sizes, some nearing the size of a dog, claimed their land. Near the rabbits, a swarm of rats and other rodents; the rats, like the rabbits, varied in size, and the family noticed even the rarest of rodents they called a capybara. As large as a dog, it seemed a giant compared to the average rodent. The different rodent species kept mostly to themselves, yet did interact with other rodents, as did all the other species.

The different monkey species and apes kept mostly to the trees—except for the gorillas at the ark—but often ventured to the open plains and interacted with the other species of animals. One by one, the animal herds ventured back and forth to the nearby water source, where Noah had been soaking the rib beams.

The next few days were much different. The animals had become used to the humans, and the humans had become accustomed to the animals rather quickly.

The family had quickly taken advantage of the more "domesticated" creatures, adding the newly arrived oxen to their workforce, along with the cows and horses.

The family noticed, to their dislike, the band of gorillas intently watching them work. It made them uneasy, and they could feel the big, deep, dark eyes of those monstrously powerful creatures glaring at them, following their every move, their every breath. The tension within them magnified when they passed near the band's claimed land. As they walked above them on the scaffolds, the gorillas watched intently, and the family continually glanced anxiously back at them.

When some of the gorillas moved closer with their loud huffs, the family momentarily froze and stared at the animals. The gorillas likewise froze and stared. This happened for the whole first day and the next.

On the morning of the third day, as the men were working on the scaffolding, they quickly became uncomfortable as all of the gorillas seemed to startle. They all stood to their feet and watched, intently, all huffing and snorting. The men stopped working several moments and glanced at each other with uneasy eyes. The gorillas calmed a bit. They were still huffing and snorting, but not nearly as much as a few moments ago, and the family returned to work, slower this time, keeping particular attention on the frightening beasts.

They were setting the last of the ribs into its proper place, fastening it to the top of the curved rib and securing it into place. Ham was leading the oxen away from the ark, as he had done countless other times.

The oxen he led were harnessed to a mechanism that held several large woven ropes that led to a pulley, which lifted the heavy wooden rib as the oxen pulled the ropes. Shem, Noah, and Japheth guided the end of the massive beam toward the wedge slot of the curved rib beneath it.

The gorillas all huffed and snorted, distracting the family as several gorillas stepped forward a few steps.

Suddenly, the pulley snapped. The oxen lurched forward from the sudden release of weight. The pulley arm fell, crashing to the ground. The giant rib came tumbling down.

Noah, Shem and Japheth hollered a warning as the massive beam tumbled down between them. Noah and Japheth stumbled and fell backward, barely dodging the falling rib. Shem, on the opposite side of the gigantic piece of wood, wasn't so lucky. He hit hard on the surface of the scaffolding as the long, giant, tumbling beam crashed right through the lower levels of the structure, destroying the support beams that held up the scaffolding on Shem's side. He and the scaffolding went tumbling to the ground.

The scaffolding that held Japheth and Noah quickly became a precarious perch, as the missing section left it unstable.

The closest three gorillas bounded forward as they saw the rope snap.

The first leaped up onto the scaffolding nearest to Shem, narrowly missing the giant beam as it plunged to the ground. The gorilla jumped up as it grabbed the second level scaffold, swung up and around onto the second level, then leaped out into the falling section of the scaffolding, grabbing a tight hold of the far support column, and swung. He stretched out his hind feet, as he swung around catching Shem in mid-fall. Pulling Shem up to his body, and holding him with his free arm, as he finished his swing, he dropped to the lower level. The scaffolding crumbled behind him. The gorilla swung around, again grabbing hold of the supporting column and swung out into the open air as the scaffolding came crashing down. The gorilla landed, hunched over, supporting itself with his free hand, and pulled Shem close to its chest. The scaffolding section crashed down hard on the massive creature's back, and it

144

huffed, grunted and snorted as the bamboo pummeled its back.

As the first gorilla raced to save Shem on the other side of the fallen rib, the other two darted up the section of the scaffolding that was precariously holding Noah and Japheth. They leaped up onto the unstable scaffolding, grabbing a supporting column and swung around, flinging themselves up onto the second level. They punched off the walkway, swinging back around the column, up and around onto the third level. The two gorillas landed almost at the same time, just as the scaffolding finally gave way and crashed to the ground.

The gorillas each snatched up the shocked and confused man closest to them and leaped up all in one swift motion. The scaffolding plummeted to the ground as the gorillas grabbed a firm hold of the top of the Ark's ribs, smacking hard into the side of the giant beams. Noah and Japheth, hanging in the free arm of their respective saviors, dangled in pure shock and awe at these magnificent beasts, unable, at the moment, to even speak as they absorbed what had just transpired.

The gorillas held tight to Noah and Japheth with one arm and climbed down remarkably fast, using only their three free limbs. They reached the ground shortly after the gorilla that had rescued Shem had landed.

Shem's rescuer held him tight for a few more moments after the bamboo scaffolding had stopped bombarding its back and released its grip on Shem.

The three men, now released from their saviors' grasps, didn't move a muscle. The gorillas each let out a huff and returned to their band, who circled around the three huffing and puffing, patting and rubbing on them as if comforting their injured and praising their heroism.

The three family members turned around to observe the damage, their hearts racing with a plethora of emotions: awe, shock, fear and excitement.

By this time their wives had all reached them, standing a few feet away, they had heard the destruction and immediately dropped what they were doing to check on their husbands. They stopped in mid-stride as they noticed the gorillas releasing their loved ones and returning to their band. By this time, Ham had also recovered from the accident and started making his way toward them. The women rushed over to their respective husbands, interrogating them with questions regarding their injuries and what had transpired.

Everyone's emotions died down a few minutes later, and the family discussed how to repair everything, of course deciding first to fix the bamboo scaffolding and set to work on it. As the family returned to their tasks (the women working on supply preparations and the men on repairing the scaffolding), the four working on the scaffolding noticed several gorillas nearing with a bundle of bamboo Noah had stacked by them, several yards from the boat.

They watched as the gorillas dropped the piles a few feet from them, unsure what the gorillas were doing. One of the gorillas snatched up a long piece of bamboo, stretched it out to Noah, huffed and nodded his head toward the ark.

Noah looked at the ark, then back at the gorilla. The gorilla huffed and nodded again. Noah gently took the bamboo from the gorilla who then knuckled his way to the broken scaffolding and started pulling at a knot that connected a broken piece of the scaffolding.

"I think he wants to help," Ham said.

"Me too," Noah replied and walked over to the gorilla.

Noah untied the rope securing the broken bamboo piece while the gorilla watched, then the gorilla held up the replacement so Noah could secure it to the scaffolding.

Noah turned back to his sons a moment, an

astonished grin on his face, before tying the new bamboo to the scaffolding.

Almost on cue, the rest of the gorilla band began snatching bamboo and following the example of their alpha. The family joined in with the gorillas and their father, amazed at what was happening.

With the help of the band of gorillas the family finished the last rib and fastened it in place. Their newfound coworkers had helped them reconstruct the destroyed scaffolding and then finish the rib. Now, they had started fastening the beams in place for the three levels of the ship.

The organization and the intelligence of the gorillas baffled the family. Things were coming along fast now that Noah's entire family were helping, as well as the gorillas. They had started fastening the beams in place for the first floor. When finished with those beams they would do the second floor, then the third.

The gorillas had become a tremendous help with their strength. They merely carried the beams and held them in place while Noah's family secured them in place. By the end of the first week, they had begun placing beams Noah had calculated they wouldn't get to for three more weeks. This was, of course, because his initial calculations had not included the gorillas' assistance.

Soon after the gorillas had joined in helping with the construction, several of the other animal kinds had started helping. The elephants first, using the strength of their trunks to lift the massive cuts. The giraffes followed, offering their necks as lifts. After the giraffes, the monkeys began helping with the lighter and more manageable tasks, and the family started to use even other animals to help with both heavy and light projects as well as using the more intelligent creatures for some of the more complex activities. Noah even gained the courage to approach the pride of lions, which he recruited to pull loads.

It seemed to Noah and his family that the great God who had called him to save the world was granting them all favor with the animals.

***

They had been working steadily and efficiently for over a week, more efficiently than Noah or his family had ever thought possible, the animals working alongside each other in perfect harmony.

Within the week, they would be a full month ahead of schedule, and Noah was excited things were going so well. After the animals had all started working with them, and the family no longer felt they needed to fear any of the beasts, they all had decided to erect tents and simply move their belongings to the area, so they wouldn't need to make the long trek to the ark every day. They had been having trouble in the city, anyway, and felt it would be safer to be among the wild beasts. They knew this to be the case because just days before they relocated, a small mob had

151

decided to try, for some reason, to attack the ark and its surrounding inhabitants. They were quickly annihilated.

Something new happened that day, a week to the day since they had moved into their tents. One by one the family felt it. It was almost unnoticeable, at first. Then it got louder and stronger. It was a slight rumble accompanied with a slight vibration, at first, and quickly grew to a loud rumble—like that of a stampede—with a vibration that started knocking small items over. Then it turned into an immense shaking and loud, roaring, cracking. The family could barely keep on their feet as the ground shook, and they had to scream over the sound of the cracking and breaking. Their hearts racing and fear paralyzing them, they stood there, never having experienced anything like what was happening as the ground a few yards from the ark lurched up, then fell away into an abyss of blackness, in a loud, deafening roar.

Then it was gone.

The family stood motionless for several moments, shock and adrenaline coursing through their veins.

The most unnerving thing, though, was the animals. They didn't notice the animals until after the quake, but none of them seemed spooked. Many of the animals sauntered casually over to the newly-formed chasm as if expecting something.

After a few more moments their nerves settled a little. They again heard roaring, but it wasn't the same sound they had heard with the shaking. As the roaring got louder, they realized what it was. It was a tumult of water raging their way. Then they saw it. It was coming from a channel made by the quake, rushing into the chasm a few yards away.

The animals gathered near the newly-formed pond and started drinking from it. The family stood, again in amazement. It seemed, as of late, that more and more, the miraculous happened. Yet, it never became any less incredible. They watched the animals a few moments as they began drinking from the newly-formed pond.

"Well, looks like we don't have to haul our drinking water anymore," Japheth said. "Who wants to be the first to try it?"

Noah made his way to the stream before it opened up into the pond, knelt and scooped up a handful of water and sipped his palm dry.

"Wow!" he exclaimed. "It's amazing, the freshest I have ever tasted!" he scooped another palmful up and drank it.

The family, encouraged by Noah's reaction, each scooped up a palm full of their own, and like Noah, scooped up seconds, and thirds and fourths.

"This *is* the freshest water I have *ever* tasted," Dinah exclaimed, and everybody nodded in agreement. After a while, they continued with their work. It comforted them knowing the animals did not consider the events of the day as anything to be concerned about, and they knew

the animal kingdom could sense much more than the

human race. They often knew when danger was near, and

they could even detect changes in the atmosphere. The

family knew the animal kingdom had another sense about

them that helped them to survive, so the family just went

about their business.

As they worked over the next couple of months

plaining the wood for the deck flooring and nailing them

onto the almost completed boat. A constant trickling of

amphibians and reptiles came steadily, mostly keeping to

the trees and the newly-formed pond at first, but as more

and more arrived they began spreading to the more open

areas, huddling in small groups.

In just a little over two months, thanks to the help of

all of the animals, they had finished half of the deck. They

had to make the inside staircase to connect the first two

levels, which didn't take long at all—a half day at most. Noah's plans for the decks was to build the rest of the second level, make the connecting staircase to the third level and finish the third level. After the decks were finished, they would make the living quarters and then work on the final touches to the boat. He estimated with about six more months of work it would be finished. Then the end of the world would come.

Cargo hold view
ot the three levels.

Noah, Japheth, Ham and Shem stood on the roof of the ark, discussing the last section of the boat: the living quarters. It seemed Noah had thought of almost everything, if not everything. The plans called for a large hearth in the center of the living quarters, so the lower levels of the ark could be heated. A pipe vent was to be added that led from the hearth all the way down to the bottom of the ship, with a lightweight fan to suck in the warm air from the top, which the animals would turn. This, however, was merely a precaution to ensure the climate in the ark stayed comfortable for all that lived in it. The living quarters themselves would be divided into four corner rooms, with a hallway stretching the length, separating the rooms and leading into a large open area in the middle, separated with only the hearth in the center. One side of the large open area Noah had marked "kitchen" and the other side he had marked "family room." The kitchen and the family room both had a staircase down to the bottom levels of the ark.

They worked on the living quarters through the next two months, masterfully fastening the long heat pipe through the three cargo levels of the great ship and putting the final touches on the ship's top deck, as well as some last-minute additions, such as nailing and securing a walkway that surrounded the outer hull of the ark so that it could be inspected from the outside for signs of damage.

Another last-minute addition was an outside trough with a pulley system to get ocean water into the ship so that it could be converted into drinkable water. The pulley mechanism was expertly designed.

Both the trough and the pulley simply extended a couple feet out from the ark with the trough at a slight angle upward. A notched wheel fastened to the deck connected a knotted rope that settled, tightly around a second notched wheel. The second wheel held another knotted rope that held a pail, tied in each of the rope's several dozen knots. These would be lowered gently over the side and fastened to another wheel at sea level, which stabilized the rope as it turned. As the first wheel was turned, the rope knots would catch in the grooves of the wheel's notches and turn the wheel. The second wheel, connected by this rope would catch the knots in its own grooves and spin as well. This second wheel would grab in its notches the second knotted rope with the pails in it and turn the rope. The pails, once caught by the wheel, would turn upside down, spilling their contents into the trough. The water would travel down the trough into a large basin where it would be transferred into barrels and stored until it was distilled into drinking water.

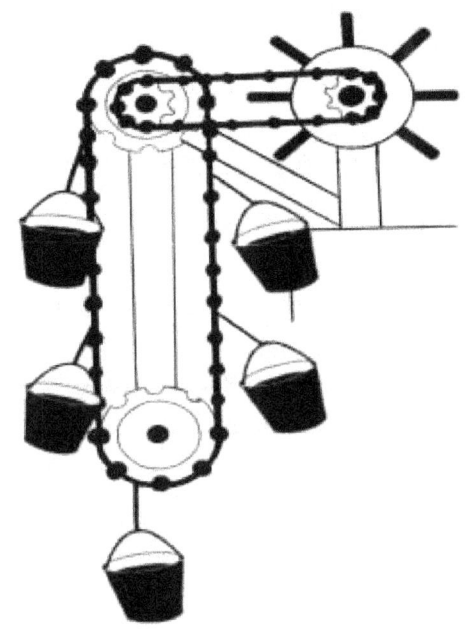

One of the last things Noah did was wall off the bottom storage section in the stern, which would be used as a refuse flush. They sealed it with pitch and made sure the exposed refuse trough vents (which most of the animal waste would flow to) sealed when closed. They decided to use a couple of barrels to catch the waste from the bottom level of the ship and dump those manually every day.

Noah had created the individual cages so that they were slightly slanted so when they rinsed the pens out the water would pool in the corner and flow down the troughs. After the cages were cleaned, and in the refuse hold area, the collected waste would be flushed by unlatching a trap door just above sea level, which allowed the refuse to spill out into the ocean.

***

Noah declared the ark finished and the family began moving the supplies into their respective cargo holds. Noah had made slabs of hardwood to put over the stairs so they could haul the supplies up on small carts rather than needing to climb up stairs. This made their jobs much easier. They started with the bottom storage section in the bow of the ship, Noah had designated this for all of the backup equipment and extra items to be stored such as soup caldrons, utensils, bedding, cloths and anything else the family thought they might need. They used the animals such as bears, oxen, horses, lions and buffalo, to speed up the process by hauling large cargo carriages. Several gorillas helped, both to load and unload the items into their transports while the smaller animals like monkeys and badgers helped to unload the lighter items.

Again, with the help of all of the animals, the work went swiftly, and they had finished the first cargo hold in no time.

After the bottom hold was stocked, they moved to the two middle storage holds. First, they stored the extra lumber, tools, pitch, nails and anything else related to boat repair or carpentry.

After they had finished the stern storage hold, they moved forward to the hold on the middle level at the bow where they stored the various animal feeds, bundles of grass and hay and dirt.

They finished the second level and moved on to the third level where the aft storage hold would store grains and other foodstuffs such as flour, wheat, honey, salt, sugar and corn. The forward storage they would use as a greenhouse, growing fruits and vegetables.

After the third level was stocked, they loaded the deck above with empty barrels for the water desalinization process.

When the loading was finished, most of the family set about furnishing their living quarters while Noah worked on the water desalinization processing units.

Noah had designed the desalinization system to work in tandem with the hearths, so each room, as well as the main family room, would have fresh, drinkable water and be able to warm the water while the hearths were on. The main hearth was intended to work almost nonstop and heat the entire ship if need be.

He had set up another trough system that would bring the water into the various hearths when opened. The hearths would heat the water in boiling chambers to the evaporation point. The condensation would then build up in a dome section as the water evaporated and then would be deposited as it cooled back into water in another container. This new container would be clean, fresh, drinkable water.

He intended to use the hearth's main warming pipe to warm the rest of the ark, if he needed to, by using several of the animals to turn another wheel that would spin a fan, sucking the warm air into the lower portions of the ark.

Noah had stocked wood and coal enough for six months if the hearths were used every day for six hours, so he guessed he had plenty. He did not anticipate having to use the hearths to heat the ship that often.

***

Noah had just finished the final touches on the desalinization system for the family room when Ham yelled for him to get outside. He set his tools down and jogged down the hallway of the living quarters, carelessly throwing the door open as he stepped through the threshold.

He didn't notice it at first but saw his family staring off into the distance. He followed their gazes and saw it.

"It's happening," Shem said in a low, hushed tone.

"No. those aren't clouds," he replied as he spun slowly around, noticing the dark black shadow wasn't just in front of them, but coming from all directions. "It is all around us and moving fast toward us." He waved his finger in a circle, indicating the whole of the darkness surrounding them.

"What is it?" Naomi asked.

"Birds!" replied Shem. "Look," he ordered as he pointed to the treetops around the ark. Hundreds and hundreds of birds had perched atop the surrounding trees.

They noticed when they looked back up, the black cloud now had white sections and gray sections. It was indeed birds.

Suddenly, a rainbow of streaks erupted before them, their hearts skipping a few beats at the sudden surprise.

"Butterflies!" Dinah exclaimed with pure joy.

Thousands and thousands of butterflies swooped up before them, in an array of colors and sizes. They looked up to see them fluttering in the sky. They leaned over the edge and saw the entire ground covered with patches of thousands of butterflies and thousands more fluttering low to the forest floor. More swooped up at them, splitting wide and skirting the family's faces as they neared.

The eight of them felt like children again, giggling and laughing as the butterflies tickled their faces

The flurry of butterflies was over just as quickly as it started, and the family stood, awed. Above them fluttering butterflies, and below them, a prism of colors as the butterflies rested and fluttered below. Several of the animals ignored the butterflies that alighted on them, and others swatted at the creatures as they fluttered by. Some seemed angry, and others seemed playful. It was truly a sight to be seen, and the family relished in the beauty of nature.

They had forgotten about the army of birds until the shrill shriek of a great bird and the shadows of the host of birds fell upon them. They looked up and saw birds of all kinds soaring through the sky, cutting paths through the fluttering butterflies, some perching on the ark itself, and others swooping down, around, and back up into the pink sky.

A great bird, again, let out a shrill shriek as it plummeted down straight toward Noah. Its white head and tail and yellow beak a stark contrast to its dark feathered body. Noah backed a few steps from the rail as the bird swooped up at the last second, made a wide circle in the air and perched on the rail right where Noah had just been standing. It stared directly at Noah and let out another shriek, then cocked its head to the side and back straight again. Its deadly beak and razor-sharp claws were a menacing and frightful sight, and none dared move. The eagle flapped its massive wings and leaped into the air, seeming to hover for a few seconds. With a mastery of the wind, it inched forward until it flew, or rather hovered, only inches from Noah, who stood frozen before the creature. It shrieked again and shot high into the air.

Noah let out a breath and looked at his family.

"It's like they know you, Dad," Shem said. "First the lion and now the eagle."

Noah shrugged.

"I can't explain it like I can't explain pretty much *anything* that has been happening lately," Noah replied.

"Well, I guess we don't need to understand, but one thing is for sure, only God could accomplish this," Naomi added, and all the family agreed.

They looked out over the ark before them, and the sight truly astonished them. Scattered among the butterflies stood thousands and thousands of birds of all kinds. Most perched on the treetops, creating a black and gray forest all around them, with several patches of white as well as splotches of color from the more colorful birds.

It was evident, however, that the majority of birds were black or gray and the forest surrounding them suddenly seemed a little more menacing than before, with the dark colors blotting out the green of the trees, their surroundings now becoming a grand display of contradiction. Animals that would typically be battling for territorial rights of the land mingled among each other, the brooding dark colors of the birds contrasting against the bright myriad of colors of the butterflies. The countryside before them, serene, yet unsettling, and as the birds and butterflies settled into their new roles among this canvas of contradiction, the dark and the bright seemed to meld in one giant panorama of brooding peace and ferocious tranquility.

Eventually, the family got back to stocking the last of the living quarters while Noah inspected the ship and its mechanics.

***

The ark was all but finished. All that remained was to place piles of hay or mounds of dirt in the cages with which the animals would make their homes.

Noah and the rest of the family were discussing how they would start filling the animal cages when they noticed several of the animals sauntering into the ark. They looked at each other with surprise and confusion, and one by one it dawned on them what was happening. The animals were picking their own cages. The first few couples to lead this migration of sorts were the lions, the gorillas, the monkeys, and the giraffes.

The lions strode to the top level, as did the gorillas, and monkeys. The giraffes stayed on the bottom level. The next few couples were the tigers and panthers, which followed the lions into the same cage. An elephant couple followed the giraffes, taking the pen opposite the giraffes, and a pair of bears claimed the pen at the stern end of the top level across from the gorillas, monkeys and baboons, which shared a stall. Meanwhile, a pair of wild dogs claimed a smaller stall in the middle level.

A steady stream of paired animals poured into the ark, some claiming a stall of their own and others sharing their cage with others of similar kind. The sheep and goats shared a pen while the buffalo and oxen shared one as well. The smaller animals claimed the smaller pens and the larger animals claimed the larger stalls.

The family was so enamored with the scene before them of the animals; the animals, of their own volition, entering the ark and the beautiful array of colors brought by the butterflies fluttering around that none of them noticed the alligator creeping up from behind.

Suddenly, Noah let out a loud cry as he fell to the ground, holding his leg, burning pain erupting in his calf. The whole family startled as he let out his pain-filled scream, then they all practically jumped out of their shoes as they noticed the alligator just feet away.

Noah, himself, scrambled away as he realized why he felt the searing pain in his leg. At first, he thought the gator had bitten him. However, upon a quick examination of his leg, he realized it must have been a powerful slap from the creature's tail.

The alligator seemed almost immediately to start walking away after tail-slapping Noah.

"What was that?" Japheth asked as he helped his father up.

"No idea, but it hurt," Noah replied.

They noticed the alligator stop and look back after a few waddling steps, then, after a few moments, it spun around and waddled back over to Noah again.

"What's it doing?" Zaphira asked.

The alligator stood there, motionless for several seconds, as did the family. Then, suddenly, it whipped its tail around, slapping Noah hard in the leg again. Noah screamed in pain and jumped back. The gator slowly turned around and took a few steps, then looked at Noah again.

"That's weird," Naomi said.

"Does it want something?" asked Shem. Almost on cue, an elephant, which had made its way over, sprayed a trunk full of water on the alligator.

Noah suddenly gasped as he realized what the alligator wanted.

"I know what it wants!" he exclaimed. "Come on, we need to add a few last-minute things to the floor of the ark," he ordered, zigzagging around animals, both big and small.

A few hours later, the four finished the last-minute addition Noah had been so excited to add, and a pair of alligators, along with some lizards, frogs, salamanders, and other amphibians soon found their way into the newly-formed small pond in the ark.

Noah had not thought to supply a pond for those creatures that would need to keep cool or need to dip every once and a while.

The day had been full of miraculous events and hard work for the family. After the animals had picked their own stalls, and Noah, along with his sons, added the small pond to the bottom of the front portion of the ark, they started hauling dirt and hay into the stalls.

The dirt mounds were for the burrowing creatures like the groundhogs and prairie dogs. The hay was for food and bedding for the other animals. It took them the rest of that day and half of the next to haul the dirt and hay.

The women worked on their own projects, such as transporting the fruits and vegetables they had been growing, as well as their own stores of soil, and water. They also finished the last touches to the living quarters and did anything else they could think of that would benefit them or make life on the ark more pleasant.

At one point, Naomi, after discussing with the other women, suggested adding more barrels of supplies to the top deck because they wouldn't really need much open space up on the deck, and if they stored even more supplies up on the deck as an extra precaution, the extra deck space wouldn't be a waste. Noah agreed, and they added more supplies to the top deck, leaving only wide walkways from the living quarters to the pulley, the water barrels, and the outside ramp.

The pulley system itself was not yet deployed over the side of the ark, for Noah had not entirely fastened it together, knowing they wouldn't need it for some time. It lay strapped to the deck among the barrels of supplies. Noah hoped they wouldn't need nearly all the supplies they had. Otherwise, they would be on the ship for a very long time.

HOLY WAR

It was the third day after the birds and butterflies had arrived that they had finally finished strapping the last of their new supply barrels to the deck. They were enjoying a relaxing meal under the open sky near the ark when the birds to the North suddenly took flight, their shrieks, and chirps slicing through the air in a chorus of shrill warnings. The eight family members knew something was wrong. The animals stomped, huffed, growled and did whatever the various animals did when they felt threatened. The air carried the scent of danger, of death. The wind held a faint cry of rage, of evil. The family stood to their feet, more sensing the danger than seeing or hearing it. They stood still, holding their breath as they strained their eyes, and straining their ears, searching and listening for what had them all on edge.

The animals were all in defensive stances, the felines, and canines with their fur up. The canines barring their teeth. The gorillas were on their knuckles and huffing. The bears stood tall on their hind legs, and the rhinos stomped their hind legs, along with the bulls.

The enemy came forth, then, with no declaration of war, no declaration of intent. They just came, like a flood, out of the shadows of the forest, a steady stream. At first, it was hundreds of soldiers in full armor, and weapons. After the soldiers, the townspeople clad in makeshift armor and farming or trade tools for weapons. They charged at a full sprint, and they were upon Noah's family in seconds. The bloody battle then ensued.

It wasn't a battle for territory, or power, or fame, but a battle between good and evil, for survival. Noah and his army were grossly outnumbered by the inhabitants of Fulstron, and both were fighting for what they believed right. The townspeople for the annihilation of all those they believed the cause of this strange demonic phenomenon, and Noah's army for the survival of the human race and all those creatures who had entered the ark.

Upon the first sight of the humans, the animals had immediately charged, in defense of everything that was good, that was holy, that was blessed.

The soldiers and citizens of Fulstron rushed from the concealment of the trees at full sprint with a roar that surpassed even that of the lion, with them, a volley of arrows arching through the sky.

Arrows struck the ground, every few feet, many landing dangerously close to the family. Those that hit their intended targets were signaled by yelps, roars, whines or whatever sounds the respective animals made as they cried in pain.

Everything was a blur of motion, of sounds and of emotions. Fear gripped the family, but with that fear came courage. Shem ordered his brothers to get all the women into the ark; then he ran headlong into battle—into what he was trained for.

The animals by this time had reached the front of the battle lines.

***

Half a dozen rhinos charged their way through the front lines, dodging swords, impaling soldiers with their horns or trampling them underfoot. Their thick leathery hide was an added armor against the blades assaulting them. Blade after blade smashed down upon their thick skin, some with little effect, others finding their mark. The rhinos took dozens of soldiers down before they were finally killed, themselves.

The first of the rhinos charged right through the front lines as if the soldiers were paper, its two weapons: the force of its power and its horn. The mighty beast trampled through several soldiers as it slammed its head into another, then jabbed its horn through the armor of a second, lifting him up as if he were weightless. The rhino wildly shook its head until the dying man flew off its horn knocking and trampling half a dozen more soldiers as it continued to charge through the enemy ranks.

Soon, however, a heavy blade found its mark, sinking deep into the creature's side. It roared in pain and spun to face its attacker, who suffered a quick death. Another soldier near the rhino noticed his counterpart's sword still protruding from the beast's side and, with what he would soon realize to be his last few moments, ran headlong into the rhino, his sword tip outstretched before him.

The rhino, again, roared in pain and spun. This soldier kept his grip on the sword and swung his blade around as the beast's head rushed in toward him, horn point plunging into his stomach.

The rhino roared in pain as the steel penetrated its neck. It stumbled as it flung the soldier off into another charging enemy. It bled profusely from its wounds and was weakening by the moment, its life force leaving its body and pooling beneath it. That didn't stop it from fighting until its very last breath, however. It managed to trample several more soldiers before the loss of blood made it collapse.

***

The band of gorillas charged into the frontlines of the battlefield managing to down half a dozen enemy soldiers before the first few fell, including the band's alpha.

The soldier who felled this deadly creature soon felt the wrath of its mate. She heard her mate's roar of death as the man plunged his sword through the creature's massive chest, and before her mate even dropped to the ground, she was upon his killer.

The soldier retracted his sword from the alpha gorilla, and as it fell, the soldier's eyes went wide with terror. He saw as the massive body of his victim dropped, opening his line of sight to what lay behind the fallen gorilla—its mate mere feet away. Her teeth bared, she moved with such ferocity and power that the soldier hesitated in pure dread, which cost him his life as she bounded toward him, jumped onto the back of her falling mate, using him as a punching board, and dove at the soldier.

The soldier barely had time to react before her teeth sank deep into the man's neck as the two tumbled to the ground.

She rolled back onto her feet as two more soldiers attempted to take advantage of her on the ground. To their disappointment neither were successful, resulting in their quick demises.

As she rolled to her feet, she jumped onto the first as he swung, knocking him to the ground with a gaping, bloody wound at the neck. She spun, barring her teeth at the second soldier. He dropped his sword and ran. The gorilla caught up to him before he finished his third step, and he, too, fell to the ground with a gaping bloody wound at his neck.

The next few moments for her would be her last, as, not only two soldiers, but five now circled her. She downed one before they were able to kill her, each stabbing cold steel deep into her body.

Suddenly, two of the four men left tumbled to the ground as a pair of lions pounced onto their prey. Without hesitation, the two remaining soldiers immediately advanced on the two giant cats as they attacked their comrades.

Just as they were about to swing killing blows, two more cats bounded up, sinking their teeth deep into the sword arm of the soldiers.

The two soldiers who the first of the lions attacked defended themselves as best they could, their swords on the ground, knocked out of their hands when they fell, and their backs exposed. They both rolled over as the giant cats clawed and bit at their leather armor. As they turned, they blocked the animal's mouths with their own forearms, protected by leather armor and with their other arm, they frantically blocked the clawing of their attackers.

The two cats leaped from their prey to the second pair of soldiers who now, themselves frantically defended against the second two lions. Soon, the two lie dead, no match for their attackers now doubled. The lions bounded away for new prey.

***

The wild dogs and other species of feral cats fought similarly, attacking in small packs then rushing off to find new victims. Even if they hadn't killed all of their opponents, they left the injured for another animal to finish off.

***

The elephants were some of the hardest of all the creatures for the soldiers to put down. The parade of elephants seemed the most ferocious. They ran through the massive crowd of soldiers swinging their heads and trunks about, smacking into anyone in their way as the soldiers sliced and stabbed at them. Some elephants had grabbed makeshift weapons: lumber, branches, even uprooted tree trunks or enemy soldiers, themselves, swinging them about, or throwing them into the enemy ranks.

The elephants, at first, ran side by side plowing through their enemies underfoot. Though they were clumsy creatures, their immense size countered their awkwardness with sheer power.

When the elephants eventually separated, the lead elephant, the largest and most powerful, along with a couple more of the more massive elephants, barreled straight into the heart of the most heavily armored soldiers, attracted by their bright metallic breastplates and helmets.

The elephant had managed to find a large, thick tree trunk as a weapon, and as it charged through the soldiers, it swung its large weapon back and forth, sending soldiers to their backs grievously injured or dead.

The weapon eventually broke and the elephant resorted to snatching soldiers up and sending them crashing into their counterparts.

For every dozen enemies, the elephants killed in this manner a half dozen more were trampled underneath, and a dozen sword blades met their marks, slicing deep gashes in their leathery hides.

The battleground among the lead elephant and its two flanking counterparts was littered with crushed or battle-broken soldiers clad in heavy armor, the three alone annihilating their enemies before a volley of arrows pierced their thick hides. Volley, after volley, after volley dug into their leathery skins, distracting them enough for several soldiers, many at the cost of their own lives, to sink their swords into the elephants' thick hides.

The elephants panicked in agony as the blades sunk

deep into their flesh, their last foes to be killed by accident as they fell, crushing those unfortunate soldiers not fast enough to dodge the falling creatures.

***

The giraffes, though not as effective, attacked similarly as well. They had no weapons except their long necks, which they used to send attackers flying through the air, and their mighty kicks, their legs deceptively weak in appearance.

Some were downed by arrows and others by swords, though none died without dispatching a few dozen soldiers.

***

The rodents—of all sizes—acted more like a diversionary squad than anything else. They clawed their way wherever they could on their enemies; under the metallic breastplates as well as the leather armor, inside the folds of clothes, biting and clawing every inch of the way.

190

The tormented citizens and soldiers soon found their ends at the face of, not the rodents, but a feline or canine, ape, bear, or another such animal.

***

The bears attacked in groups as well, ensuring maximum lethality. For every bear killed, several dozen soldiers met their dismal end with a torn throat or clawed out chest.

As with all the animals, for every one death, a half dozen more of the enemy met their fate. Even more died after the army of trained soldiers had been dispatched, save a handful, and the townspeople now became the primary targets. With the untrained civilian army, the slaughter tripled as the animals devastated the enemy ranks. Eventually, the townspeople fled back into the safety of the forest and their homes as the newest of their enemies arrived, effectively decimating any hope that they would or ever could win in one last wave of attack that evoked such terror in the townspeople ending the battle mere minutes later.

***

The birds, like the rodents, acted as a diversion, clawing at their foe's faces with the occasional success of snatching an eye or two before another beast finished off their opponent.

***

The monkeys of all kinds stayed to the trees. They received the worst of the attacks. Yet, their sheer number offset the scores of deaths. They were late to the battle only because they kept to the high tree branches, and though they moved with lightning speed, they had to circle around the open fields to get to the massive army.

When they finally reached the lines of archers, most of whom had stayed in the safety of the trees, the archers immediately started picking them off with arrow after arrow, most of which found their marks. For every monkey that penetrated the enemy lines, the archers felled a dozen.

They attacked, as would be expected from the outside edge of the archery line. The archery line itself stood three men deep before the monkeys arrived, each taking turns firing their deadly missiles into the newest of their foes. As the monkeys began attacking the archers searched the trees for the source of the shrill shrieks that echoed through the forest from this new army. Instantly, upon seeing this new flanking army, they began firing.

Within minutes, hundreds of dead, dying, or injured monkeys of every kind sprinkled the ground, their number outnumbering the fallen enemy 5 to 1.

Those that hadn't fallen by loosed arrows attacked with a crazed frenzy, dispatching an archer for every two monkeys killed by melee combat.

Though the number of archers was cut by a third, the monkey army was all but annihilated, and they returned to loosing bolts into the open field.

A third of the archers in total ventured out into the open field amidst the army and so were spared the onslaught of monkeys, but many suffered similar fates as those around them had from other animals.

***

The battle ended soon after the archers returned their attention to the fields, with a horror that melted even those with a fortitude of steel.

Millions of insects, arachnids, and reptiles flooded the forest behind the archers. They realized too late the terror before them, noticing only moments before they were engulfed by this new wave of deadly creatures. The rustling of grass, and leaves, and the buzzing of wings, a roar that grew so quickly that by the time the archers turned to face their new foe the creatures were mere inches away.

Seconds later, the screams of the dying men muffled into silence as bees, wasps, ants, snakes, scorpions, spiders, and the like crawled, flew or slithered into their mouths, stinging or biting every inch of their bodies. The victims tried to scream out in pain, but the instant they opened their mouths from whatever creatures were consuming them, their mouths filled with the creatures. Some swallowed the creatures as they panicked; others shut their mouths in a futile effort to keep the cloud of insects out. Both ended up dead, arachnids and insects burrowing into their lifeless corpses, their bodies blistered and motionless. Their deadliest foe swarmed into the open field like a wave moments later. More enemy townspeople fell to their deaths, their screams muffled into silence. Seconds later, even more fell. Wave after wave, townspeople dropped in muffled screams as clouds of insects engulfed them, and rolling waves of spiders, scorpions and other arachnids swallowed up their prey.

As the townspeople and few soldiers left in the battle arena began to notice what terror awaited them, without hesitation, they dropped their weapons and fled.

Many still found their deaths at the hands of this newest army, and many more found their deaths at the hands of the animals. In the end, few of the townspeople of the great city of Fulstron survived.

***

Shem and his brothers were near the very rear of the battle lines, and they were tiring quickly now, having dispatched many foes with the help of the animals. They had snatched up swords from fallen soldiers and joined in the battle as some enemy soldiers broke through the defending animal lines. They fought with skill they didn't know they had; Shem even surprised himself, surpassing even that of his training as a Legionnaire.

They all noticed, then, that their foes had all began turning tail and running. Then, they saw why, and it terrified even them, though they knew they were in no danger.

The sky before them was patches of dark clouds,

and the ground was alive with a moving skin engulfing everything.

They dropped their swords and stared in terrified amazement.

Moments later, the last of the townspeople of Fulstron disappeared into the safety of the trees. The insects, arachnids and reptiles scattered, most returning into the forest with a handful making a new home in the depths of the ark.

Noah, who had stayed with the women in the safety of the ark, snatching up a spare board for a weapon in case anyone made it into the ark, led the women out, only to be horrified with not only the devastation of life around them but at the newest inhabitants of the ark casually making their way past them. They froze, only to dart away seconds later as the insects, reptiles and arachnids disappeared behind them.

With the danger now passed, the family stood

among the bodies—bodies of both beast and man.

The field they had just days before seen as beautiful and surreal, now was appalling and horrific. Hundreds of animals lie dead, scattered throughout the battlefield among hundreds, maybe even thousands of lifeless men. Both animal and man alike were brutally killed, their blood marking the land with pools and streams of dark crimson.

The family could not put into words the loss they all felt as they saw the animals lying dead, with blood matted fur and lifeless. Of course, they felt sorrow for the men, but none could honestly tell if it even neared the sorrow for those animals they now called friends.

After several long moments, Noah somberly walked over to the nearest body, a deer, and started dragging it away from the ark. The rest of the family watched, at first, then began helping with the other bodies. They piled both man and beast in the same pile until it was waist high with corpses, and, just as in every other task, the surviving animals helped as well. They dragged or carried the lifeless bodies of both man and beast into the mass graves.

The day was a sad one for both Noah's family and the animals, as they spent the rest of the daylight hours and much of the night clearing the field of the dead. When it was all done, Noah set the piles on fire. The family watched for several minutes and, one by one, entered the ark.

They had started sleeping in the living quarters now that they were finished, and settled in quite well, using the family room and kitchen as they would when they would be at sea.

The next morning, the family made their morning patrol of the ship to make sure everything was in order, and they noticed several more species of creatures had made the ark their home. Bugs of all sorts had nested in the walls and the cracks of the ark, along with insects of all kinds, such as beetles, ants, spiders, caterpillars, bees, grasshoppers and others.

WORLD'S END

After the family had finished their morning preparations, they chose to eat down on the ground again because they all knew they soon wouldn't have the option to enjoy a picnic on nice grass. Although there were ominous piles of human and animal bones and the grass was still stained with blood, it still was a rather peaceful and surreal sight with all of the birds, butterflies and animals roaming—at least if they had their backs to the piles of bones.

They had finished their meal and were enjoying their pleasant surroundings, finally not having any projects to work on, when the pink sky darkened for just a second. They all looked up toward the sun to be partially blinded as the sun reemerged from behind whatever it was that had blocked it out. They lifted a hand to shield their eyes from the blinding pink sphere.

They heard a loud thundering noise getting louder. Then, they saw it—a giant streak of white light racing across the sky, pointed at its tail and fat at its front, like a flame, only burning brighter and more terrifying.

The thundering quickly became so loud it was deafening, and the family squinted to keep this streak of light from blinding them as it soared past. The thundering faded to a bearable level as the fire in the sky soared away, leaving a cloud trail behind it. Seconds later, the family heard a crashing boom, louder than anything, and unlike anything they had ever heard before.

Japheth's dog startled at the noise and darted off into the nearby trees.

"Sarid, get back here!" Japheth ordered.

They felt something else, then—something wet and cold—something nobody on earth had ever felt before.

Rain.

It started as a slight drizzle, gently padding everything with drops of water. Then it grew into an all-out pouring. Thick, hard drops pounded at the clothes and flesh of the family, splattering everything with water.

Nobody had to say anything. They all knew it had begun.

"We need to get into the ark," Noah ordered as he started gathering the picnic supplies.

"I'm going to get Sarid. I'll be right back," Japheth said and darted off in the direction Sarid had run off.

The family snatched up all of the picnic supplies and raced into the ark.

***

Japheth raced through the thick brush, calling out for Sarid. He knew there was little chance the dog would hear him, and he didn't know why Sarid was the only animal to get spooked by that boom after the fire from the sky passed, but at least he had to look for him. Japheth had begun to realize things happened for a reason, though he had no idea what the reason could possibly be for Sarid being the only one to spook.

He thought for a second; maybe, he was not supposed to join the rest of his family on the ark.

The rain wasn't as bad under the canopy of trees, but it still fell hard and thick. It had only been minutes since the rain started and the ground was already being enveloped in places by pools of water.

He felt tremors, now, much like those that had happened when the pond had formed near the ark. He knew, though, this was much, much, different. He could sense it, feel it even. The ground beneath him shook violently, and he stumbled into a tree, grabbing it for balance. Then, suddenly, a small explosion erupted a few feet behind him, followed by a loud hiss as a cloud of white shot out from the ground. He could feel the heat from it, steam, boiling hot steam. It mixed with the cold rain as it shot into the air, making the rain warm.

The shaking subsided enough for him to keep his balance, and he continued his search for his friend, his dog. As he ran in the direction he last saw Sarid disappear, he saw more and more of the steam fissures burst into existence, and soon there was a constant hiss surrounding him.

He knew he didn't have much time, and just as he was about to give up, he saw Sarid. Sarid stood at the opening of a tree trunk whining and pacing.

"Sarid!" Japheth yelled above the hissing and growing rumbling, as he rushed to Sarid's side, noticing a litter of puppies.

"Oh, boy. Is that why you ran off? Where is the mommy?" he asked as he looked around the area, then bent down. He bent low, quickly unlacing his shirt, and gently snatched up the four puppies. He noticed one very small, almost half the size of the rest, and another almost twice as large, and with much longer legs than the rest. He gently tied his shirt around the four puppies in hopes of securing them inside so they wouldn't fall out and cradled them in his arms.

The ground shook so violently that Japheth fell to his back, and the air erupted into a deafening roar. He saw several trees fall a few feet away and decided not to wait for the shaking to subside before trying to get back up.

He struggled to his feet, the ground shaking and the roar still deafening, and half-ran, half fell in the direction of the ark, Sarid at his heals. Trees fell all around him, and he heard loud cracking, even above the roar. He knew that cracking was close—very close.

He ran as fast as the shaking, unsteady, tumultuous terrain would let him. Then a large crack formed in front of him, and the ground before him crumbled under his feet.

He fell hard on his face, the makeshift bag of puppies falling to the ground a few feet away with yelps.

Sarid leaped into the air as hard as his canine legs would allow as the ground fell from under him and Japheth.

Japheth started to slide backward—backward into a great fissure—the ground under him sliding and crumbling away. He frantically searched for something to grab onto, but there was nothing, nothing but brush and grass. Thorns poked into his hands, arms and bare chest, but he didn't notice.

Just before the last of the ground fell away from under him, a section to his left crumbled, revealing a system of roots connected to a tree still standing. In a last-ditch effort, he reached for the roots. His hands slid freely on the roots' moistened surface, and he knew this was the end. He would not make it back to his family, his wife. Then a hand caught, and he stopped with a shoulder-jarring jolt.

He noticed, then, the ground had quit quaking, and he pulled himself up the root, kicked his leg over the edge of the broken earth and peered down into a deep canyon. He had no measure of how deep it was, only that if he had fallen, it would have been to certain death. He pulled his upper body over the edge and crawled several feet from the precipice before he stood.

He looked back at the canyon, wanting to see what had almost taken his life. When he saw it, he stood in awe at the canyon—a grand canyon before him. It stood miles in every direction, he knew. He could see the trees on the other side, only as a blanket of green.

He only stood for moments before Sarid reminded him of the danger, and he snatched up the makeshift bag of puppies and raced toward the ark again.

***

The family had quickly finished gathering everything they needed from the picnic as well as anything else they had left outside. After everything was inside, everyone but Zaphira ran about the ark making sure any loose items were fastened to something. Zaphira stood at the door waiting, waiting for her husband to return. Every moment that went by caused hope that he would return to fade, especially after the rumblings and the quaking. She stood for what seemed like hours as the rain beat down hard on the ark and began filling the open field with large puddles. The puddles grew and grew until the whole field looked like a lake.

Finally, she saw him emerge from the tree line. A minute later, he passed through the threshold with Sarid and the puppies, falling to the wooden floor, gasping for breath.

The family all had returned to Zaphira's side by then, and as soon as Japheth had entered, they began pulling on the ropes to raise the ramp that doubled as a large door.

Seconds later, the door was shut, and again the family was astonished at what happened. It confirmed in their hearts that they were acting according to the will of their God when the door seam started glowing a bright orange diminishing only seconds later with no seem. God had fused the door to the rest of the ark's hull.

Shem helped Japheth to his feet, and they all heard a loud explosion accompanied by a quick and powerful rumble. They looked at each other, and Shem darted for the stairs. The rest of the family followed in close pursuit.

They all burst out onto the deck of the ark and saw what had made the tremendous noise and shook the ground. A mountain off in the distance had seemed to expand and blow its top. A dark cloud formed over the mountain and a bright red flowing substance oozed from its peak like the earth was bleeding. The family stood there, watching it— the bleeding mountain—as the earth's blood flowed and spewed out of the severed peak. They had never seen anything like it before, had no idea what to make of these happenings—except it was the end, the end of what had been and the beginning of what would be—a new world.

From every direction, sounds of exploding geysers erupted, and the water rose even faster. The earth began to shake almost constantly, and then they saw the flood rapids erupt from the surrounding mountain region.

The mountains off in the distance seemed to crack in half, their peaks crumbling and water spewing up high into the sky as if the crumbling mountains were releasing their rage on the world below. The water's force broke apart what was left of the mountains, sending some rocky fragments spiraling through the air, others simply tumbling down the weakening mountain walls.

The family watched in horror as the world before them transformed from the peaceful, beautiful surroundings they had known all of their lives into the violent, destructive, and deadly scene before them. Every time they thought it couldn't get any more terrifying, something new and more devastating emerged from the angry earth.

The mountains in the distance were now reduced to piles of sunken earth and stone, and the erupting geysers were now less menacing. The family released their grip on the rails of the ark's deck, only to grasp the rails tighter than ever before seconds later.

The ground shook the ark with great fierceness, and the family feared it would not only dislodge the ark from its supporting beams but tear the ship apart.

The rising water below them began to recede. It fell fast, faster than they knew it should have. None said a word. None dared move. None dared even look at another. They all knew something terrible was about to happen. Then it did happen—more terrifying than anything they could have thought of and more horrific than anything they could have imagined.

They knew it was miles away, and they knew they

were in immediate danger. They hoped it would diminish before it reached them, and they stared at it, paralyzed with fear.

Miles away, where the old mountains had been only minutes before, a single mountain mass, the size of which none could fathom, erupted from below the depths of the watery surface. It seemed to span dozens, if not hundreds of miles.

What terrified them, though, beyond the sudden formation, beyond the past few moments of all that had happened, was the massive wave heading their way. They didn't see it at first, but as it grew closer, it grew larger. That was when ultimate fear gripped their hearts. The wave seemed to grow ever larger as it neared. The family's ever-increasing fear grew. None could take their eyes from the wall of doom as it rushed closer. The roaring was faint at first, but it grew with the wave's size as it neared.

The wave was upon them, a wall of water that

drowned out all else in their sight, its call a roar of

impending death.

Then it happened.

Something they didn't expect.

Something miraculous.

Something only the Creator could have

orchestrated.

The deadly wall of water broke, its roar died and it

passed harmlessly under the boat with only a slight jostling

of the stilts holding the ship in place.

The waters all around them still raged, and though

this giant wave seemed harmless to those in the safety of

the ship, they knew it was deadly to those not in the

sanctuary of the the ark.

They had no idea how long they stood on the deck

of their great ship. They only knew the devastation they

saw, men and women surrounded the ark now, banging at

the hull for the family to let them in. They knew the

townspeople were screaming, but the sound of the raging

earth drowned out any voices. One by one, those outside

the the ark drowned—some because the raging rapids

smashed them into the the ark itself, or another object, and

knocked them unconscious. Others, now treading water due

to its depth, simply sank in exhaustion. Still others were

carried away, conscious, struggling to survive the deadly

currents that were now the world.

The family of eight stood on the deck of the the ark,

leaning on the rails and watching in horror as the waters

raged, the lands shook, the newly-formed mountain erupted

and the rains poured down. Below them, men and women

of all ages surrounding the boat lay motionless, cold, blue,

lifeless, bodies of men, women, children and infants.

Suddenly, the boat shook violently as several of the

many beams holding it secure buckled under the stress of

the rushing waters and those clinging to them for survival.

The eight held tightly to the railing, fearful the ship would overturn. The rainwater, which had only just begun falling, had already risen over the roofs of several houses, and the family could feel the waters drifting the boat from its resting place. Finally, after several long and tense minutes, the ship broke free of its anchoring supports. Rocking uneasily back and forth, it floated freely with the currents of the water.

Following the many currents from the many destructive forces that had so abruptly changed the face of the world, the ship took them through what was left of the city they had called their home. Huddles of people gathered together on the rooftops of buildings that had not yet been devoured by the waters. Noah and his family held on for dear life as the currents led them deeper into the remnants of their former home, and the family looked on in amazement at the torrents of waters that flowed from the surrounding mountain regions sweeping through Fulstron. The currents seemed to gain in strength and fury as they swept through the rubble of the once great city and converged throughout the ruins into great roaring rapids.

The unfortunate souls atop the various structures near the converging points of the rapids were easily and mercilessly swept away. The buildings were battered into remnants of their former glory or beaten down to nothing.

The enormous and bulky ship carried its crew through the raging rapids, made even worse by the buildings that still stood in the water's path as the converging currents crashed into the solid structures, seeming to gain momentum. They narrowly missed several large buildings and saw dozens of trees uprooted as more water flowed over them and cut sideways around another towering structure.

Their hearts sank in desperation and fear as they saw the massive building looming before them, the town capital. Giant billowing rapids raged every which way as they splashed against it. The tallest, and largest of all structures in the city, and the pinnacle of the city's creativity and architecture, now the object of their wrathful destruction.

They neared the capital building, headed straight for it. The current was taking them directly into the massive building.

Noah now disdained his ancestors' legacy looming before him. His family line's greatest accomplishment now his family's instrument of destruction.

A massive rock that could only have been hurled by the giant mountain that now lay behind them struck the town capital, demolishing more than half of the building, sending shards of debris in all directions.

Only one wall remained, its opposite wall disintegrated by the rock missile, and the walls to its sides now half destroyed. The ceiling above was still intact, but crumbling.

The current took them, now into the half-destroyed

town capital, the water rushing in the now opened building seemed to propel the boat even faster.

The family stood frozen in fear, their knuckles white, their clothes soaked and stuck to their bodies as they passed through the crumbling structure. They passed only inches away from the edge of the broken wall. They passed the marble staircase that rounded the edge of the wall and spiraled out into what used to be massive ballroom floors. The staircase now simply stopped in midair, as the flooring and the rest of the steps had been destroyed. They passed through the center of the building and then out the other side, stone and marble crumbling all around them as the weakened building was bombarded by the torrent of water surrounding it. Finally, as the the ark passed across the threshold, the capital fell into the depths of the ocean beneath it.

Those few seconds seemed like hours for the last survivors of the human race. Yet, when it was all finished, and they passed the town capital, how they did not know, they couldn't even remember what had happened.

Their minds now driven to numbness, they continued through the rapids for several more minutes. The waters no longer seemed as ferocious and deadly; then it was suddenly calm. Just as quickly as they started, the rapids had stopped. The waters were a gentle, soothing, calm, smooth as glass. Then the family saw it. Ultimate terror engulfed them suddenly as they realized where they were.

The fleeting waters carried them across the lowest point of the surrounding mountain regions. The lowest point led to a valley at the end of which was a sheer cliff. Their eight minds churned with thoughts of their doom and destruction. The eight each envisioned their own demise, plummeting into the watery depths of the valley below them, the splintered pieces of their ship scattered about and the animals frantically swimming until exhaustion took them. They imagined themselves crushed by the weight of the heavy ship on their backs as they splashed into the water.

They closed their eyes, having no desire to see their own ends, and awaited their fate.

The family felt the ark's front end dip low as it reached the fall, and the eight braced themselves for the freefall. It dipped more, and finally, the family felt themselves go over. For a split second, the family felt as if they were floating, then felt the drop. A second later, the eight heard a splash, then felt a spray of water and a heavy lurch of the ship. They opened their eyes in surprise and shock, and they all burst into laughter.

They looked around, filled with elation and relief.

"Yeah!" Japheth screamed.

"We're alive!" Shem reported excitedly, and they all rejoiced. After a few moments, the family finally assessed that they were no longer in danger of the rapids as they surveyed their surroundings, finding nothing but calm ocean for as far as they could see. Noah suggested they inspect the ship.

Noah checked the outside while Ham inspected the bottom level; Shem, the middle; and Japheth, the top level. Dinah inspected the hold on the bottom level; Marriam, the two middle level holds; and Zaphira, the top two holds while Naomi inspected the living quarters.

Despite the tumultuous journey through their city, nothing had been destroyed or broken. Things (and animals) had been jostled, and some items had to be put back in place, but everything seemed fine overall. When the family met up again, they reported their findings to each other and took the next few hours to relax and enjoy their first meal at sea.

FIRST DAYS

Their first night at sea was difficult for all of them. It could have been the fact that every living being on earth was dead—except for those in the ark. Or it could have been that they now were the last of their race who carried a great responsibility, and it weighed on them. It could have been just that it was their first night at sea. Though the boat was too big to feel it rocking, it was different sleeping on the ocean.

They grudgingly woke and readied themselves for their morning chores, their one, true desire, to go back to sleep. Naomi worked at preparing the morning meal while Zaphira and Marriam managed the fruit and vegetable garden after they straightened their rooms. Japheth, Ham and Shem inspected the stalls, as well as the ship's inner hull for any leaks while Noah inspected the outside of the hull and the above-deck supplies.

Once their morning inspections were finished, they sat down in the family room dining area for a meal of rice, beans and bread. After their meal, they began the rest of their daily chores, which consisted of flushing the waste into the refuse hold and feeding the animals. This would only take a few hours each day, especially since the whole family took part in the "after breakfast" chores, as they called them. The most difficult section to clear refuse from would be the bottom because they would need to manually scoop up the excrement into barrels when the water cleaning gathered it into the end of the waste trough.

Noah wasn't going to bother starting the water desalinization process yet because he knew it wouldn't stop raining for quite some time. A week prior, his God had appeared to him in a dream, or a vision. He wasn't sure. God had long curly hair and a full beard, and he seemed to emanate light. He had told Noah that in a week's time He would send the rain. Just as he had promised, the rain came exactly a week later. The man in his vision also told him it would rain forty days and nights, so Noah knew they wouldn't need the still until the rain stopped.

Forty days, to the hour, the rain stopped. It was somewhere around midday, as far as the family could tell, and the rain stopped as suddenly as it had begun. They had all gotten used to the rain, and now that it had stopped, everything seemed eerie. They had gotten used to the constant pounding on the ship's roof above their heads. They had gotten used to going outside and immediately being soaked from head to toe. They were used to staring out into the vast ocean and seeing the constant sheet of water and how it mixed with the ocean as it slammed into the surface, sending ripples out into the oblivion. They had gotten used to the constant cloud cover that blotted out the pink sky, leaving only a dim pinkish-blue hue (they had noticed after the rain started that there was a blue hue, for some reason, in the pink sky) throughout the daytime hours. When night came, they had to have lanterns to light their way. That took some getting used to.

It was quiet now, outside, and the family sat in the common room eating their midday meal. They immediately noticed the rain—or the lack thereof.

"The rain stopped," Ham said flatly.

"Well, looks like I can start cutting some windows now," Noah commented.

"Windows?" Marriam asked.

"Yeah. I figured when the rain stopped I would make some windows, get some more light in here, as well as down in the lower decks," he replied.

She nodded.

"Good. Maybe we won't have to use those lanterns we installed down there as much," Japheth said.

"We'll need to start filling those barrels with seawater and start using the still, also," Noah informed.

"Great," Shem replied, "another chore."

"What's wrong, brother, all this manual labor getting too much for you?" Japheth mocked.

"Well boys, I'm going to go enjoy the weather outside," reported Zaphira as she stood, grabbing her dishes. "Anyone care to join me?" she asked.

They all glanced at each other.

"Yeah. Why not?" Naomi replied snatching up her dishes. The two women scraped their scraps into a pail near the large hearth and gently sat their dishes on the counter in the large kitchen. The rest of the family followed suit, and they all headed outside.

They were all surprised at what they saw. The clouds had quickly started dissipating, and the sun shone through several clear areas, but the sky was no longer pink. Beyond the cover of clouds stood a light, soft blue sky. The once giant, pink, glowing orb, was now an eye-blinding yellowish-orange.

"The sky! It's blue!" Naomi exclaimed. "Why is it blue?" she asked.

"I don't know," Noah replied, "maybe to remind us of what happened."

"Look at the ocean," Zaphira said. "It's so calm now, and beautiful."

"Well. It is a new world," Noah replied and wrapped an arm around his wife. Ham, Shem and Japheth followed suit, and the family of eight stood there on the top deck of the the ark admiring the new beauty of their new world at sea.

After a while, one by one, the couples began about their daily routines. The afternoon was their down time when they didn't necessarily have scheduled chores, but sometimes they went about their evening chores early. Usually, though, they would either seclude themselves in their rooms or mill about the common room, enjoying the company of the family.

Noah added filling the barrels with seawater and managing the mill to the rotation of jobs. The family agreed they would rotate job responsibilities every few days to relieve the monotony.

Noah took to adding windows to the ark for more fresh air and a breeze. After cutting the holes, he fastened leather flaps Ham had provided from his shop when he started helping, to the windows to shield against the weather if it got too cold. He tied them down to nails he set protruding from the wall. He and his family had noticed that since they had been at sea, the nights sometimes became unusually cold. He knew if the weather continued to fluctuate this much, they would soon need to use the heating hearth—even in the bowels of the ship—to keep warm.

THE TRIAL

Ninety days had passed since the first rains, and the family had started to get under each other's skin more, and more—specifically Japheth and Shem.

"He gets me so mad!" Shem exclaimed to his wife.

"I know, but you can't just go off on him like that," Mirriam replied.

"I just get so tired of him commenting on how I'm not used to this manual labor," he complained as he sat on the bed. "He's done it ever since I started helping when we were on land. I'm about ready to punch him!" Marriam sat down beside him.

"Believe me when I say I know exactly how you feel. In fact, it seems that not a week goes by that I just want to strangle him sometimes."

Shem chuckled. Shem had, indeed, remembered several occasions over the past few months when Japheth had almost gotten a scolding at the least, or a bruised body part, after one of his antics.

His brother was a child at heart, and he played childish games that got under everyone's skin. It had not been so bad when they each had lives of their own and didn't see much of each other, but now that they lived together and saw each other daily, things tended to be more noticeable.

"We just need to remember that this whole thing—" she waved her hand around the room, "—is only temporary, and someday we won't be stuck here anymore."

Shem huffed. "I hope this isn't our final lot in life," he replied.

"Now, are you ready to get back out there and finish the chores, or are you going to stay in here more and stew?"

"I'll be out in a minute," he reported and fell back onto the bed. Mirriam nodded and left their bedroom. She glanced around, but didn't see Japheth, and went back to her evening chores. Japheth had learned quite well when to leave people be and let them cool down.

The ladies shared in their job of growing the fruits and vegetables, as well as cooking. They also helped with inspecting the cargo holds, as well as emptying the refuse hold when it was nearly full.

They were all in the garden, as they called it, and were busying themselves with exchanging some of the soil with new soil from one of the barrels they had in storage. They mixed some soil with a bit of animal waste so the plants could get all the nutrients they needed to produce.

They really didn't know how the plant life survived the first forty days. The sky was overcast and very little light seeped through. This was the only place where there were initially windows, but that didn't seem to make a difference then. Now, though, with the new sun shining down, the plants were flourishing. They constantly had to discard excess eatable as well as the uneatable parts as they pruned. So they kept the best and tossed the rest in a pail for the pig slop. Food was in abundance in the ark, it seemed. Any left over from themselves, or the other animals, would be devoured by the pigs or goats, and the spices and grains were not yet halfway depleted.

While the ladies worked in the garden, and the men worked in the "stables" as they called them now, Noah worked above deck. It was his rotation to ensure the water basin was full and the barrels were emptied into the water desalinization mill.

The process for desalinating water that Noah had come up with, what he believed to be the most effective use of his time, was to empty the first barrel into the mill, then rotate the freshly emptied barrel to the very back and move all the rest in line forward. After that, he would fill the barrel from the water basin, and as he waited to empty the next barrel, he turned the pulley device turning the rope with the pails to dump seawater into the extended trough that flowed into the water basin. He, of course, always finished filling the basin before the mill had emptied.

He noticed a large, dark cloud far off in the new, blue sky. He looked around the sky near him, noticing only the puffy white clouds in every other direction. He kept an eye on that dark cloud throughout the day, whenever he was above deck, and as it grew closer and bigger, he noticed streaks of jagged white or blue light shoot out from the cloud into the water. As quickly as he saw them, they were gone. Then he saw more and more. It seemed the streaks of light came at intervals, and they frightened him, but he knew he and his family would be safe—safe because his God had told him they would repopulate the earth. His faith, though, didn't mean he wouldn't be scared—only that his fear was unwarranted. After all, he was only human.

The day neared its end, and the dark, ominous clouds were over them now. The whole family stood above deck, staring, and though none would admit it, their hearts were struck cold with fear. The waves were sloshing the boat around, and the animals were, themselves frightened: moaning, or huffing, or whining, as the ship rocked back and forth. Normally, the ark was much too large to be affected by the ocean's waves. However, the dark clouds brought with them unbearably heavy winds and frighteningly large waves. The clouds sent down, regularly—almost constantly now—a steady barrage of the strange streaks of light. The light streaks, themselves weren't the most frightening of the events, but rather what accompanied them. Every time one hit the ocean, it seemed, a loud crash boomed through the air. Light streaks, booming, and a giant wave, all brought the family into an experience they had never imagined, and they were all terrified.

The ship swayed sideways, and the family of eight had to grab the rails to keep balance.

"I think I'm going to be sick!" Zaphira said above the noise of the storm.

"It's getting worse!" Ham said.

They all had noticed it; the rain seemed even more ferocious than when the world had been flooded. It came down in sheets, falling diagonally and felt almost as solid as pebbles, freezing them to the core as the drops of ice cold water hit their skin. Their clothes were soaked through and clung to them, flapping heavily in the powerful wind.

Another wave rolled under the ship, this one even bigger than the last; and Naomi, unprepared, fell to the deck floor, slid a few inches, then slid a few inches back the other way as the wave passed.

Shem quickly grabbed her arm and helped her up as another wave passed under.

"They're getting bigger!" Noah hollered through the noise of the storm.

Indeed, the waves were getting bigger, but no one replied or even acknowledged Noah's comment, though he knew they had heard him. Not only were the waves getting bigger, but they were getting closer together as well.

Soon, the storm had gotten so violent the family could barely hear anything above the wind. The rain, hard and ice cold, brought fresh sensations of burning as each drop pelted down on them. The ark was itself a constant swaying dance as it drifted in and out of swells and crests. The boat, entirely at the mercy of the sea, followed the currents and eventually had turned so it passed over the waves diagonally. This was the only reason the boat had not capsized when some of the larger waves had hit them.

The first of the big waves came as a surprise. None of them had ever experienced a storm, let alone one of this magnitude. They felt their already unsure footing angle upward as the front of the ark rode the massive wave to the crest. The family held on for dear life, and any barrels not tied down slid, and fell to their side, rolling toward the back of the boat.

Shem didn't see the barrels until they were almost on top of him. Four barrels were rolling at him with deadly speed. He had moved from the side of the rail—as had the rest of the family—to a more secure location. He chose to wedge himself between two barrels fastened tightly to the rail.

The other seven members of the family, safely secured elsewhere, all saw the barrels on their path to devour their loved one. They yelled frantically. However, a massive, thundering crash erupted, drowning them out, their voices lost in oblivion.

Shem's eyes grew wide as he finally saw the four barrels racing toward him. He scrambled to get out from between the two barrels that now signified his doom, rather than his protection. The first barrel slammed into him, then the next two, and finally, the last. To Shem they didn't feel like four barrels; they felt like one massive barrel crashing into him. Luckily, the barrels he had trapped himself between took the brunt of the impacts. The wind was knocked out of him, he felt splinters spray his body, and the small of his back erupted with pain as the railing dug into his back. Then he went over the edge.

It seemed to the rest of the family, the very moment Shem fell, that several streaks of light burst through the night sky and shot onto the front of their ship. They all felt a massive jolt, unbearable pain erupting throughout their bodies, and they all knew that excruciating pain would be the last thing they would ever feel.

None of them understood what had happened during the light strike. Nor did they understand how they were alive. None of them had ever experienced pain like that. All they knew was that after a few moments of pain all was black. Then, the horrifying crashing sound jolted them awake. They didn't know how long they had been unconscious, but they all suspected it was only seconds.

The next thing they saw horrified them beyond experience; not because it was some terrible creature, or even a loved one dead, but because what they saw meant they might all very well perish and everything they had striven for would have been for naught.

As if of one mind, they all leaped in unison from their places of security and onto the unsure footing of the deck.

The ship had now begun its descent down the other side of the massive wave's crest, and so their footing shifted, and they half fell, half ran toward the very thing that struck horror and despair into their hearts.

One by one, they rejoined together as they half ran half fell, using each other to help steady themselves.

"We have to use the water barrels to put it out!" Noah ordered as he pointed to a tied down section of barrels. They all nodded and made their way to the barrels.

Despite the torrential downpour, the fire started by the light strikes grew slowly, but still, it grew. The ship had leveled out, now in the swell of the next wave, and the family took only seconds to open the barrels of water and dump their contents in the direction of the fire.

It only worked partially. The base of the fire that had been on the deck sizzled out instantly. However, the fire had spread to the wall of the living quarters by now and was climbing. Adding to their dilemma, the ship's front end again angled upward, sending the family to their backs, searching for something to grab onto. All but Mirriam were within reach of something fastened down, so she went sliding—sliding in the same path the barrels that sent her husband overboard had taken.

The family watched as yet another loved one plummeted into the depths of the raging sea. They had no time to pause, though, like they had no time to pause for Shem. They struggled to their feet in a desperate attempt to try to put out the fire climbing the wall. Noah suddenly had an idea. He hollered for Ham and Japheth and pulled himself over the edge of the water basin. Immediately, his two boys followed, understanding his plan.

They all knew the seconds mattered, for the fire still grew, and the ship neared the peak of the wave's crest and would soon fall the other way. They needed gravity to work for them. The three men sat in the water basin up to their necks and kicked as hard as they could at the wooden edge of the basin. Finally, after several kicks, the wood gave way, and the three men tumbled out, along with a full basin of salt water. To their luck, the water splashed against the wall enough to stop most of the fire, and the rain took care of the rest.

Noah, Ham and Japheth all slid across the ark until they slammed into more fastened-down barrels on the other side. Then, the ark crested the wave and fell down the other side, sending the three men sliding back the way they had just come.

Noah was able to stop himself by grabbing the wall of the living quarters while Ham maneuvered himself so he could grab onto the safety rail. Japheth, however, wasn't so lucky. He slid right into the water basin, slamming hard into its opposite wall.

They noticed the next few waves seemed a little smaller, the wind lessened slightly and the rain didn't seem so ice cold. With the subsequent waves smaller and the fire doused, the family remembered Shem and Mirriam.

Shem and his wife lay on the outer walkway they used for inspecting the outer hull. He had fallen over the edge and was able to catch himself on the railing, and when he saw his wife slide off, he caught her, slowing her descent enough that she could grab the railing as well. He had almost fallen over the rail when he grabbed her. He thought that would have been ironic. They hunkered down there, keeping a strong hold of the railing supports so they didn't fall off. Once they felt they could safely manage their way back up on the deck, they started their slow ascent. The storm was still overhead, and footing was treacherous with the constant shifting and wet wood, so they went slowly.

The rest of the family returned to their places of safety to wait out the rest of the storm, their hearts heavy with sorrow as they grieved in somber silence, the loss of their loved ones. The storm was a fitting environment for how they each felt.

Of course, they all jumped to their feet when they saw Shem and his wife emerge from the ramp gate at the rear of the ship, without concern for the unsure footing and rushed toward the two of them, overwhelmed with joy that they were not dead.

That concern was quickly remembered when the ship shifted again, and they all almost lost balance. They each snatched a good grip on the rail, and with a new zeal in their hearts, seemed to forget the storm and give an account of what happened after their separation.

After the storm had calmed enough for the family to walk safely, they began inspecting the ship. The women started in the living quarters, picking up everything that had been knocked out of place, which was almost everything. They first cleaned the common rooms, and then they cleaned up their own bedrooms.

The men all went below deck to inspect the stalls and the animals. They did find several stalls in which the larger animals dwelt with parts of the railing destroyed. However, the animals didn't seem to mind. No animals had been injured, but many of the flying insects and reptiles buzzed or slithered around, still unnerved by the storm. Some of the animals expressed their nervousness with their own calls or grunts; but, overall, none seemed badly disturbed or injured.

The family slept in the next day, all exhausted from the past night's experience. When they finally did wake, Ham and Shem went about the morning routine while Japheth and Noah worked on repairing the water basin.

When Noah and Japheth had finished, they started their own morning chores, and because the two of them were farther behind in their chores than the others, Shem and Ham helped pick up the slack after they had finished.

When breakfast was prepared, they were caught up, but still several hours late, due to their sleeping in, and so they had only a short recess from their work after their late morning breakfast. It was too late to eat a proper lunch, so they skipped lunch and had only a small snack; then worked their evening chores and ate a rather large dinner afterward. By this time, they were all famished and devoured their meal, the wives gracious enough to cook a smorgasbord of beans, rice, potatoes, bread, cheese, milk, juice, various fruit cuts and vegetables.

The family gorged themselves on the buffet, leaving few leftovers, and forewent their usual rituals of winding down before bed, going straight to their rooms after cleaning up.

DOWNTIME

A couple of weeks had gone by since the fire, and the family had been at sea a total of one-hundred five days, now. Things had become monotonous and tedious for the family, so they started filling their free time with newly invented games and experiments, to keep themselves from going insane.

They each had taught themselves to swim since they were surrounded by water and they hadn't much else to do. Noah was the first to do this, as he daily inspected the outer hull of the ark. By now, he had gotten used to maneuvering himself around the walruses, and the seals and whatever other seafaring creatures managed to find their way onto the ark. On occasion, he would see some debris floating, and one day he had decided to attach a rope from the ship to himself and enjoy the water for a change. He had never needed to learn to swim because there were not many bodies of water near where he and his family had lived. He soon learned to swim and didn't need the rope. After helping to teach the rest of his family, they had regularly begun taking swims, and whenever they saw debris on their down time, they would race to it or make up other games involving it.

Occasionally, other seafaring animals would surface near the ark, sometimes even while one or more of the family were in the water.

For Noah and his family, it seemed these creatures that often lounged above deck felt just as much like family. At first, they had thought the walruses, seals and other animals that found their way up onto the ship were always different ones, but soon they noticed the same marks on the animals and realized the creatures were following the drift of the ark.

This particular day, Noah had noticed some driftwood with a particular sea lion relaxing on it, and as it was during their downtime, he called for the rest of the family for a game. A few minutes later, the seven maneuvered their way through an obstacle course of animals and neared Noah. The family, almost immediately understood what Noah had intended when they saw the sea lion. This particular sea lion had a lighter streak from one front flipper to the other front flipper across its back. It sat on the driftwood, now barking out its sea lion's call as it noticed the family.

"Stripes wants to play, huh?" Shem asked as he came up next to Noah.

"I'm thinking sneak and grab," Noah replied as he nodded toward Stripes.

Stripes had maneuvered so that he lay on his back with his head facing away.

"Ah, I see," Shem replied.

Stripes turned his head toward the family and called out, then turned back away.

"Well, better not leave him waiting," Shem said and leaped from the ramp rail into the water with a loud splash. Noah followed, as did Ham.

Upon hearing the splashes, Stripes flung his head around momentarily, then after seeing the three swimming toward him, turned his head away. He lay perfectly still, the three members of the family quietly closing in.

The three silently swam up behind Stripes. Noah lifted a hand, pointing three fingers up. He folded one down, then a second. The next moment the three lunged— or at least, the equivalent of a lunge when in water—with a splash, at Stripes.

In a flash, Stripes rolled onto his flipper and leaped into the ocean's abyss, the three men not even coming close to touching the sea lion.

"Where did he go?" shouted Ham as he frantically searched the water around him.

"I can't see him!" Shem replied, doing the same.

"There!" Noah hollered and dove into the water; a blubbery bobbing head disappeared under the water.

"I almost had him. I touched him!" Noah exclaimed in triumph as he reemerged from his dive.

They trod water, searching for the creature. Seconds passed with no sign of Stripes. Then a scream and a splash erupted from the ark.

The wives and Japheth sat on the railing of the walkway watching. They saw the three cautiously swim up and dive at Stripes, who, lightning fast, disappeared into the water. Then Noah dove, and they heard him boast of his almost-successful attempt.

None of them saw the seal come up behind them and pad over to Mirriam. No one had any warning when the seal leaped the few feet onto the rail beside Mirriam, balance for just long enough to brace itself against Mirriam, and push. Mirriam let out a scream as she fell into the water, the seal with her.

The three men treading water turned to see the commotion. Mirriam splashed up from under the water, the rest of the family laughing and a seal calling out next to her. Stripes took advantage of the distraction and struck. He leaped out of the water, like an arrow, soaring over Noah's head and came pummeling down onto Ham.

Ham barely had time to turn his head and hold his breath when he saw the creature. He was so fast, as Stripes barreled down on him. He went under, the heavy creature on top of him. Just as quickly as Stripes was there, he was gone.

Mirriam splashed up from under the water, the seal next to her, her family laughing. She retaliated, diving for the creature that had knocked her off her perch. The seal vanished under the water before she even got near it.

The seal reemerged behind her and rolled its heavy body into her. Again, her family renewed their laughter as Mirriam spun around only to find empty air. The seal bobbed its head up out of the water just long enough to be seen and disappeared.

"Here, Mirriam. Let me help you up," Japheth said as he hung his arm over the edge.

Ham splashed up from the water's surface, taking in a deep breath, Noah and Shem laughing. Stripes bobbled his head up behind Shem for several moments.

"Shem!" Ham exclaimed as he pointed. Before Shem could even turn around, Stripes leaped out of the water and smacked his flippers into Shem's back, pushing him down. Shem bobbed under the water, his assailant vanishing.

The leathery hide of Stripes rolled up from under the water in front of Noah, accompanied by the familiar sea lion call. Noah dropped a hand on Stripes.

"We can never catch you, can we?" he said. "We are getting tired," Stripes seemed to understand and swam to the ark, followed by the three men.

By this time, Mirriam had successfully climbed back onto the ark and was now drying off.

The family stayed out on the walkway for a while longer, and eventually, everybody got in the water for at least a little while. The days were pretty warm, but the nights were cold, so the family had started using the hearths, but Noah hadn't started using the main hearth to warm the stables. The animals didn't seem to be cold, so he left the fan wheel unused. Maybe it was because of the sheer number of animals in the stables that kept it warmer at night; he wasn't sure, but they seemed just fine.

The days, though, had become very warm, and often they just sat outside, enjoying the warm breeze between their daily chore routines.

***

Japheth swung open the door to the cargo hold where the grains were stored, led Zaphira in by the hand,

256

and once she was inside, shut the door behind them in a hurry, both giggling like children.

Japheth kissed her, pulling her close as he guided her into the cargo room.

The passion was thick in the air, and the excitement was intense. Neither of them had ever done anything like this, and the fact that they could get caught excited them even more.

They kissed and walked; Japheth led his wife into the dark corner, neither able to see well in the dark cargo hold. The little light that shone through the slits near the roof added to the feeling that coursed through their bodies, the darkness adding mystery, and the slivers of light adding a sense of forbidenness.

Zaphira's back slammed into a support beam, and she let out an exhilarated huff as the sudden jarring sent another sense of invigoration through her. Japheth smiled, noticing the lighting seemed to highlight all of his wife's best features: her skin, her eyes; her curves and a rush of desire flooded through him. He kissed her again.

Zaphira leaned against the support beam, Japheth kissing her hard, passionately.

"This is exciting, isn't it?" Japheth said between kisses stretching his eyes wide.

"Unbelievably," she replied as she kissed him back, unlacing his shirt.

Japheth pulled himself against her, pressing hard against her body. He ran his hands up under her blouse, feeling her smooth skin. He kissed her. She pulled him tight. Zaphira pulled Japheth's shirt off over his shoulders. It hung half-on half-off his back as his arms, fully engaged in wrapping around his wife, kept the shirt from finding its way to the floor. Japheth pulled his wife's blouse off her shoulders, bringing it up over her head and arms, dropping it onto a barrel next to her, exposing her bare skin.

Zaphira pulled him close to her feeling his skin on

hers. He kissed her neck, his body pressed against her.

She grabbed him, clawing at his back. He kissed lower.

The door swung open, letting in the light from the main stables of the ark. At the entrance stood Ham, frozen in something between shock and embarrassment. Zaphira snatched up her blouse and covered herself with it, and Japheth stepped back, pulling his shirt back on.

After a few seconds, Ham cleared his throat.

"Umm, I need to, uh, get a few," he lifted up several small spice boxes, "spices, for Mom." He cleared his throat again.

Japheth nodded, Zaphira looked away. Ham awkwardly shuffled to the corner that held the few spices he needed. A minute later, he was gone, not saying a word.

"Well, uh," Japheth said as he stepped close to her again, bringing his arm around her waist. She knocked it down.

"Are you crazy? What if he comes back, or someone else comes in?"

"He is not coming back," Japheth said, "and isn't that the whole point, the danger of getting caught?" he said in a hushed voice as he brought his arm back up to her waist and leaned in for a kiss.

Zaphira smiled mischievously and dropped her blouse.

The next meal was especially awkward for Ham. He rarely even looked at his brother, and practically refused to look at Zaphira, and he wasn't as talkative as usual. He was acting noticeably uncomfortable.

Japheth and Zaphira, being the only two who knew why, kept flashing each other smirks when catching each other's glances.

Dinah was the first to notice Ham's behavior and commented. He blamed a lack of sleep or something, evading the question. He didn't want to make things any more uncomfortable for him than they were now. He wasn't really sure how Japheth and Zaphira would react to him spilling the beans on their love affair in the cargo hold; they might get embarrassed, but he did know he would be even more embarrassed if he told.

He had definitely walked in at the wrong moment. He knew if he had walked in just a few minutes earlier things wouldn't have been as awkward for him.

He had seen more than he should have, he had seen too much of the bare body of another man's wife, let alone his brother's wife. To make matters worse, he had always found Zaphira beautiful, and he felt even more uncomfortable around her now *because* she was beautiful. He had seen more than he should have.

He knew he hadn't done anything wrong, as well, and he knew Dinah would understand the situation, but he couldn't help but feel like he had betrayed her in some fashion, and he didn't want her to know…exactly how much he had seen of Zaphira.

Throughout the rest of the meal, he tried to act normal and succeeded in keeping the suspicions that something was going on with him to a minimum. Though he knew Dinah did not believe his excuse, she let it go. He still didn't look at Zaphira, though, and he made it a point to avoid her as much as he could for the rest of the day. When he was around Japheth, he ignored the situation and just acted as if he had never caught the two of them in the cargo hold, and things got back to normal with him and his brother rather quickly.

***

That night was warmer than usual, and Shem had brought his wife above deck to spend a nice romantic evening with her. He had set up a small picnic behind some barrels near the edge of the boat, and they sat staring out into the black sky, their arms around each other.

"This new black sky is just beautiful, isn't it?" Mirriam commented.

"It sure is. I like this sky better," Shem replied, as he squeezed her close. She put her head on his shoulder.

They sat a few moments, her head on his shoulder, his fingers gently gliding back and forth over her hand and between her fingers.

"It's been a while since we have come out here," Shem said.

"It has," Mirriam replied.

They saw a tiny streak fly across the night sky.

"Did you see that?" Mirriam asked.

"Yeah, crazy. What was that?" Shem replied.

"A star," Mirriam answered

"Moving? A moving star." Shem replied.

"A falling star," Mirriam said.

"A falling star," Shem replied. "That sounds better." He smiled.

They heard a noise behind them and turned to see a little black monkey with a white patch of fur on its eye.

"What's he doing out here?" Shem thought aloud, more to himself than to Mirriam. "Hey, Patch, come 'ere, come 'ere Patch," he called to the little monkey.

The monkey immediately obeyed and climbed up Shem's arm, resting on his shoulder. "Hey boy, what are you doing way up here?" he asked as he scratched its belly.

"I'm going to go take him back. I'll be right back," he said and kissed Mirriam, then jumped up and disappeared into the living quarters.

Japheth hid in the shadows, Patch on his shoulder. "Okay, boy," he said, and waved his hand toward Shem and Mirriam, who sat on a blanket, looking up into the sky.

The monkey jumped off Japheth's shoulder and made its way toward Shem and Mirriam, and a few moments later, he heard Shem enter the living quarters. He waited a few more moments and turned around to face a massive, solid black gorilla, patting it on the chest. "Your turn. Remember, be quiet," he whispered as he put a finger to his mouth. The gorilla mirrored the gesture and quietly— as quietly as a several-hundred-pound gorilla could be on a wooden floor—made his way toward Mirriam, Japheth following.

Mirriam sat forward, looking up at the sky and all the stars that sprinkled it. She was always amazed at the number of stars visible in this new night sky. Before, there were far fewer stars. Now, there didn't seem to be a spot that didn't have a star in it.

She heard "Shem" come up behind her. "That was quick," she said as she stared up into the night sky. She was about to turn around when he didn't answer, but then she felt his knuckles massaging her back—she didn't notice how large his knuckles were. "Ah, that feels good," she said, focusing on the starry night again.

Japheth stood mere inches behind the gorilla covering his mouth, his face turning red in silent laughter. It was all he could do to keep from exploding in laughter.

"Shem" brought a hand up to her hair, gently stroking it. She closed her eyes, enjoying the love her husband was showing her—again, not noticing how large his hands were.

Japheth dropped to his knees in silent laughter, one hand covering his mouth and the other on the floor for balance. He tucked his head down, his face red.

"Shem" brought a heavy hand down onto Mirriam's shoulder, resting it there for a few moments. Mirriam brought her own hand up, resting it on his. She felt rough, leathery skin she knew not to be Shem's and looked down to see, in the corner of her eye, a solid black, monstrous hand. Immediately, she jumped away and, upon seeing its owner, let out a loud scream of surprise and fear.

At that moment, Japheth couldn't hold his laughter in. Since the jig was up, he burst out into hysterical laughter, falling on the floor, as the gorilla backed away several feet, startled by Mirriam's scream. Seconds later, the door to the living quarters burst open, and Shem came racing out, followed by the rest of the family, all in their evening wear.

Shem was just coming back up the stairs when he heard his wife scream and immediately sprinted through the living quarters. The rest of the family had been jolted awake by her scream as well and darted out of their rooms, racing down the hallway right behind Shem.

The gorilla, now more startled by the sudden appearance of the rest of the family, started huffing loudly. It looked back and forth at all of the family, then Mirriam, then the family at the entrance, then Japheth. It backed away, unsure of what was happening.

Mirriam, having figured out what was going on the moment she saw Japheth laughing, recovered from the shock of seconds ago and charged at Japheth, who was still on the wooden floor laughing so hard that he could barely breathe. She pounded on him as hard as she could while he lay laughing, curled up in a ball to protect himself, unable to stop laughing, despite the abuse.

Noah, Dinah and Zaphira pulled Mirriam off Japheth as soon as they saw her assaulting him. All of this excitement and sudden movement made the gorilla even more nervous, and it began huffing loud enough now that the rest of the family noticed its behavior.

Ham cautiously stepped between the family and the gorilla, slowly moving closer. The gorilla stepped back another step as it noticed Ham.

"It's okay," Ham said in a hushed voice as he put a hand toward the gorilla. He took a couple of slow steps toward the massive beast. The gorilla huffed, its full attention on Ham, now that the initial ruckus had come to an end. "It's okay," he said again, taking a few more steps. "Come here."

The gorilla huffed one last time but stayed where it was. Ham took one more, slow step. The gorilla didn't move, only stared at him. Ham took one last step, slowly, and gently touched the palm of his hand to the gorilla's chest. The gorilla stood still for a few more moments, then put a powerful hand on Ham's forearm. Ham brought his arm down and opened wide for a hug. The gorilla stepped in, picking Ham up off his feet in a hug, and the gorilla let out a series of friendly huffs.

"Okay, boy," Ham said with a chuckle. The gorilla put Ham down. "Let's get you back down to your stall before you get upset again, eh boy?" he said and grabbed the gorilla by the hand, leading him around the living quarters, away from the commotion of the family, so he wouldn't get upset again, and through the far door to the living quarters, through the hallway, down the stairs and into its stall.

Once Mirriam had been pulled off Japheth, he slowly stood to his feet, still laughing, but not as hysterically as before.

"What did you do?" his wife asked harshly. Japheth stopped laughing at this point, but chuckles slipped through every once and a while.

"I trained Midnight to…" he chuckled, "to act like a human."

"And pretend to be my husband!" Mirriam shouted. Japheth chuckled again.

"Yeah, it was hilarious!" he replied, letting out a snicker. At this, Mirriam went mad with rage. She lunged for Japheth, fists flying, but Shem had taken hold of his wife's waist. Knowing the extent of her anger, Shem strengthened his hold on her as he felt her lunge for his brother.

Japheth jumped back, barely dodging her fist.

"Let me go you bastard!" she yelled to her husband as she ferociously attempted to elbow her husband behind her and wiggle free of his grasp.

"I am going to kill him! Let me go!"

Shem, at that point, picked his wife up and half-walked, half-staggered around the corner out of sight.

The rest of the family could hear the two arguing, mostly Mirriam threatening both Shem and Japheth and Shem trying to calm her down.

"You sure can be a jerk, sometimes," Zaphira said and walked around the corner. Japheth heard Zaphira tell Mirriam to leave with her and stop thinking about her bastard of a husband.

Japheth knew, then, he had disappointed his wife.

The rest of the family just walked away, all with scowls on their faces as Shem rounded the corner again, his wife calmed by Zaphira.

"Why the hell do you do things just to get everybody mad!" Shem scolded. "You need to grow up. You are nothing but trouble. That's all you ever have been! Always playing tricks on people! Nobody likes it— nobody! You need to stop and think about growing up!"

Japheth just stared at his brother as Shem scolded him, knowing it was better just to listen and not say anything.

Shem slammed open the door to the living quarters and stopped.

"By the way, I wouldn't talk to Mirriam for a few days," he informed and slammed the door behind him.

Japheth knew he had taken his joke too far almost immediately when his family had all rushed through the doors and the gorilla had gotten spooked. Still, he had a tremendous laugh. He would just avoid Shem and Mirriam as much as he could for the next few days—especially Mirriam.

He walked over to the ship's edge and admired the night sky.

Everybody was mad at him this time, not just the ones he had pranked; so, he knew he had better stop the pranking for a while—and apologize.

Japheth chuckled again, as he stared out into the new black sky and watched the new clouds cross the new white moon.

He stayed out on deck for a while, waiting for everyone to get settled into bed again, then turned in himself.

The only thing his wife said to him as he bundled under the covers before she turned away from him, was, "Are you happy with yourself?"

It bothered him that she was angry with him, more than everybody else's anger at him, as it would any spouse if the other was upset with them.

***

The next day, Japheth could feel the tension in the air from the minute he woke. His wife did not speak to him during the meals and even the chores. The meals were the most tense, as he could almost sense the anger emanating from Mirriam. When he asked for some item near her to be passed, she grabbed it and slammed it down closer. Nobody said anything to her, of course, because they undoubtedly felt she was entirely justified. Japheth had both scared and embarrassed her, and though he was the only one to see what had actually happened, the family was involved, which embarrassed her more.

Nobody said much that meal, nor the next, and the chores were lonely for him as he avoided everyone that morning.

He did find Shem and apologize to him during the chores to which Shem nodded. He warned Japheth not to apologize to Mirriam just yet because she would probably slap him. Japheth nodded in understanding and avoided Mirriam the rest of the day.

Their final meal that day he apologized to the family as a whole, emphasizing his apologies toward Mirriam the most. The family voiced their acceptance of his apology, encouraging him not to prank anyone for a while. Mirriam merely nodded.

Japheth took the nod for what it was: an acknowledgement that she knew he was sorry, but she still hadn't forgiven him for making her look a fool.

The next day, things seemed like they were back to normal with everybody but Mirriam, which Japheth understood. After all, she had been the butt of the joke. The next day, even Mirriam seemed to have warmed back up to him, so things were going well—for a little while, at least.

Shem had apparently started coming down with some illness, so he was working a little slower than normal. Japheth had been asked to help his brother finish the above-deck chores so all the chores would be finished before their morning meal. He shuffled around the various marine animals that now made the ark their home.

"Well, big brother, your little officer's body just can't take this manual labor, can it?" Japheth commented as he neared.

"Shut up," Shem replied as he moved a penguin with his foot.

"Hey, it's not my fault you can't handle real work," Japheth replied in jest. "So, what do you need help with?" he asked.

Shem coughed. "Nothing," he said angrily.

"Aww, what's the matter?" Japheth began in a mocking baby talk tone. "Shemey-Whemey get his feelings hurt?"

"That's it," Shem answered, as he let go of the barrel he was rolling on its edge. He spun, his fist coming up into Japheth's stomach. Japheth doubled over in pain, the air knocked out of him. "Who's the weak little punk now, Japie-Wapie?"

Japheth's anger flared, and he tackled his brother. Already hunched over, he simply opened his arms and tucked his head to the side. Lifting Shem off the ground, he clumsily carried him several steps, smashing into several water barrels, barely missing the scattering, blubbery residents of the ark as they darted away to the safety of the sea.

Shem brought his elbow down between Japheth's neck and shoulder, sending his brother to the ground. Shem caught himself with his feet as Japheth's grip loosened. Japheth, however, brought his hand around into Shem's leg, knocking it out from under him. Shem fell to his back, hard, as Japheth, lightning fast, scrambled to his knees.

Before Japheth could tackle his brother again, Shem quickly brought a leg around to kick Japheth in the chest. The kick only partially contacted, as Japheth dodged the brunt of the attack shoving Shem's leg out of the way.

Shem used the momentum Japheth provided and continued into a full spin to face his brother square on.

Japheth recovered from blocking Shem's kick, but not before Shem leaped at him. The two collided and rolled, slamming into the wall of the living quarters with a loud thud.

Shem pushed himself away from Japheth, who had taken most of the jarring impact against the wall. "You are always messing with people!" Shem yelled.

Japheth replied with another tackle, this time using the wall to push off. Again, the brothers collided, but Shem sidestepped as the two met and used his brother's momentum against him, as Shem shoved him away with all his might.

Japheth practically flew through the air, head first into another barrel, barely bringing his arms up in time to shield his head from the impact. Japheth stumbled back to his feet, his eyes filled with rage.

Shem stood calmly, anger still boiling within. "You'd stop if you knew what was good for you," he snarled.

Again, Japheth replied with another tackle. This time he made sure he connected fully, and the two, again, went tumbling into the wall of the living quarters. This time, Japheth rebounded off the wall more quickly than Shem, who took the brunt of the collision. "You think you're better than everyone else because you were a Legionnaire," Japheth sneered and swung at his brother as Shem stood to his feet.

Shem easily dodged the swing and retaliated with a jab to Japheth's side. Japheth dodged his brother's blow as well.

Japheth charged again. This time Shem didn't bother to try to dodge, and the two tumbled to the ground. Both brothers, now in a blind rage, just kept pounding on each other as they rolled all over the deck.

By this time the family had discovered the fight due to the crashing against the living quarters. They stood shocked at first, then started calling out for the two to stop.

They did stop, but not because the family had wanted them to. The two, masked in a cocoon of rage and adrenaline, were oblivious to anything other than their own rage and the object of their anger.

Japheth eventually connected a good fist to Shem's face, which broke the rolling tangle

Both jumped to their feet, and Japheth charged his brother. Shem, again, used his brother's momentum against him and ducked right as Japheth neared. He grabbed Japheth's leg and straightened back up as fast as he could, throwing his brother back as far as he could.

Neither brother realized how close they were to the ark's edge, and when Shem saw the look on his family's faces and didn't hear the immediate thud of his brother hitting the floor, he knew something was horribly wrong.

He spun as he heard the splash, realizing, then, that he was mere inches from the guardrail. When he set his hands on the rail, he felt something warm.

Horror filled his heart, as he looked down and saw blood, and without another thought, Shem stepped onto the rail and leaped off the edge.

Japheth struggled against unconsciousness as he plummeted into the water, a fresh wave of pain erupting in his already throbbing head, as the salt water stung his wound, saving his life. The sudden eruption of fresh pain brought him back from the brink of unconsciousness long enough for him to stay afloat for his brother to reach him.

His mind was a blur, and he struggled against the blackness. The last few things he saw were a blurry form splash into the water a few feet away, then Shem calling out to him as he wrapped his arm around him. Everything went black after that.

Shem hit the water and immediately swam back up to the surface toward his brother. Seconds later, he was by Japheth's side.

"Japheth, I'm here! It's going to be okay. Japheth, stay awake. I got you, brother."

Noah saw both of his sons in the water, Shem struggling to keep his brother above water. He sprinted into action, slapping Ham on the shoulder and pointing as he darted away. Ham understood and raced down the walkway, hurriedly dodging the sea creatures that now called the ark their home.

Noah ran as fast as his legs would carry him, found the rope he knew to be lying around there someplace, and snatched up one of the boards of wood piled on the deck. Some extra wood that, as of yet, they hadn't needed to use.

He leaned it against the living quarters wall and stomped on the center with all his might. It broke in half. Noah immediately started wrapping the rope around the wood piece, tying it off so it would not come loose, then grabbed the remaining rope and hauled it to the edge of the ark. He tossed the rope and wood piece over the edge as hard as he could.

"Shem!" he yelled. "Grab the wood!" Noah turned toward Ham. "Ham, grab the rope!" he yelled down to Ham, and once he saw his son's attention on his rope, he dropped it down.

Ham successfully caught the rope in hand and tied it to the rail.

Shem saw the wood and paddled his way to it. When he grabbed it, Ham started pulling in the rope. When Shem neared the boat, Ham reached down and took hold of Japheth, who was still unconscious. Once Ham had a secure hold on his brother, Shem climbed up onto the ramp, and the two pulled their brother out of the water.

They carried him up the ramp and into his room. After a few minutes, they left Zaphira and Naomi to tend to his wound.

Now that the excitement had died down, Shem disappeared back down onto the lower portion of the ramp, wanting to be by himself, not even bothering to change into dry clothes.

Mirriam found him a few minutes later and sat beside him. He never even looked at her.

"Want to talk about it?" she asked.

"No," he replied, then coughed. Mirriam sat in silence beside her husband a few minutes, then left, resting a hand on his shoulder for whatever comfort that might be worth to him.

She heard him cough again and wondered if the wet clothes were something she should worry about, as he was already under the weather. She chose to ignore it, knowing Shem was not in a mood to receive any suggestions.

Japheth woke, his head pounding. He had slept for several hours, and when he awoke, there was a parchment on a stand next to the bed. He groggily snatched it up and read it through eyes that were not yet fully awake. The note simply said to stay in bed and take it easy. Someone would be in to check on him soon.

He did as ordered and just lay there, mostly because when he sat up his head throbbed and found relief in lying down. Eventually, his wife came in to check up on him.

Shem didn't know how long he had sat out on the railing, and he really didn't care. Eventually, a penguin waddled down beside him, snuggling with him. It gave him little comfort, though comfort him it did.

He finally left the solitude of the walkway, figuring the meal had been long over and continued his daily chores.

He had been behind when Japheth had come to help him, and now he was further behind because of the fight, as well as working slowly that morning. He started with cleaning up the mess they had made from the fight; then he emptied a couple of water barrels into the desalinizer and started filling the backup from the water basin. He took his father's idea, and while waiting to refill the distiller, he worked on filling the basin with seawater with the pulley device.

As the day went on, he worked slower and slower, coughing more and more and worked in shorter intervals between resting. By lunch, he was feeling downright lousy, coughing almost constantly, and simply exhausted. The family noticed and commented several times on his health until he finally told them to stop bothering him about it and that he would be fine. The family didn't think much of his sourness, understanding that he wasn't feeling well and that he was surely still upset at throwing his brother overboard. He asked about Japheth, and the family brought him up to date on his situation—aside from a terrible headache, Japheth seemed fine.

He was still behind in his work and continuing to fall even further behind as he felt increasingly worse as the evening progressed. Ham came up to check on Shem and help him finish up his chores. The moment Ham came into view, Shem dropped to the floor. He had been resting, and as he saw his brother, he stood to his feet and then fell right back down and lay there. Ham immediately rushed over to his side, calling out to Shem. Shem was awake but didn't seem to be able to focus well.

"I don't feel so good," he said as he lay on his back.

"All right, brother. It's time you definitely get to bed," Ham replied.

"But...I'm not...finished," Shem replied, struggling to get the words out.

"We'll worry about that later. Come on," Ham said as he hefted Shem to his feet. Ham wrapped an arm around his brother and set Shem's own arm around the back of his neck so Shem partially supported himself with the arm. This also gave Ham an additional grip to hold his brother up. He practically had to carry Shem and struggled with every step to keep themselves upright.

Shem seemed almost at the point of passing out and was clammy to the touch, yet much warmer than he should have been, and Ham could see beads of sweat on Shem's forehead. He noticed as well that Shem seemed to be coughing nonstop.

When Ham finally reached the closest door, he banged on it hard until someone opened it. It was Naomi, and as soon as she saw them, she immediately put a shoulder under Shem's free arm and helped Ham get him to his room. She called for Noah, who rushed to their side, taking over Naomi's job as Naomi held the bedroom door open, Mirriam right behind them.

"He's burning up," Noah said. "Mirriam, get a wet cloth." Without hesitation, she darted out of the room, returning moments later with a soaked cloth in a bowl, while the three got Shem into the bed and undressed him.

Nobody was concerned about the above-deck chores not being finished that night; they simply tended to their loved one. After a while, Naomi suggested the family go to bed and that she and Mirriam would stay up with him. The family reluctantly agreed.

For the first night, the chores ceased, and they all felt restless, even in bed. None of them slept well, and Mirriam and Naomi stayed up all night with Shem, trying to keep his fever down. They didn't say much, both women's minds filled with concern for Shem. They continued to dab his forehead with the wet cloth and drip water on his chest in hopes of keeping him cool. They had removed the blankets and sheets from his upper body so they only covered his lower half, again, hoping to keep him a little cooler.

He didn't look like he was resting well at all, to them. He moaned often in the night and turned his head back and forth on the pillow. He never seemed to be conscious enough to speak, but twice he seemed to come out of his feverish sleep, opening his eyes, then drifting off again.

When the sun crested the horizon and morning came, Naomi left to make a tea she had used for years to help speed the recovery of ailments.

When she returned, Shem had awakened from his fever-sleep, and Mirriam had fallen asleep, leaning on the edge of the bed. She did not look comfortable. Naomi immediately went to Shem's bedside, noticing him awake and lucid.

"Here," she said as she held out the warm cup of tea, "Drink this. It will help you to feel better." Shem didn't say a word but merely lifted his head slightly. Naomi quickly brought her free hand around behind his head for added support. He sipped slow sips for a couple minutes, then drifted off again. Mirriam never woke.

By this time, the rest of the family had started waking. One by one, they crept in to see how Shem was doing. They started to discuss how things were going to get done while Shem was recovering, and they all agreed to take shifts looking after him. They decided to freeze the work rotation until he was better and all just start the above-deck chores when they had finished their own chores. This, of course, gave them a lot less free time during the days, but nobody really cared.

Naomi gently woke Mirriam up and told her to go to sleep in Noah's and her bed while Shem was sick. She groggily did so, clumsily stumbling into their room before she willingly collapsed into a deep sleep. She was asleep before her head hit the pillow.

Zaphira took the first shift caring for Shem while the men worked on the chores and Naomi made breakfast. After breakfast, Naomi napped most of the day away in the common room while Zaphira took up the slack for both Mirriam and Naomi's absence in the daily chores.

After the morning chores were finished, Ham relieved Zaphira. Then, when it came time for the evening chores, Dinah relieved Ham. Then Japheth, during dinner, and then Mirriam relieved him for the first of the night shift. Finally, Naomi ended the cycle with the last shift. The next morning it started all over again. Noah periodically stopped by to relieve whoever was caring for Shem, to give them a little break, and to see how his son was doing.

This rotation continued for almost a full week before the family started to relax on the caretaking, as Shem seemed to be doing a little better toward the end of a week, though he still was suffering from fever. He often fell back into the fever-sleep, though he stayed awake much longer now.

By the middle of the second week, his fever was gone, and he no longer suffered from the fever-sleep, but he was by no means well. At this point, though, his family let him eat in the common room, and stroll above deck for a while. They felt he needed to recover more before returning to work, and by the end of the second week, he was as good as ever.

The family was relieved, both knowing that Shem was well and that their workload was back to normal. The past two weeks had been trying for the family, and now that things were back to normal, they seemed closer than ever. They had all, somehow, bonded closer together through this trial.

Japheth was soon back to pranking, though he never pulled anything as outrageous as the gorilla incident, and the family even seemed more patient with him and his

antics.

DANGEROUS CARGO

The family had been at sea now a total of 150 days, and over the last few months, they had noticed several of their cargo had gotten pregnant. A few had actually given birth. None of the family knew the gestation period for many of the animals, so they didn't know if the animals had gotten pregnant on the ark or if they were already pregnant before entering, but the family had started noticing several animals had begun to show, their bellies bulging.

The past several weeks, since Shem had recovered, life on the boat had returned to normal. The family continued their monotonous duties, each finding their own things to do in their free time away from the family, as well as enjoying the others' company. Today, however, their 150th day on the boat, their routine was interrupted.

It started out like all of the others. The family were all in the middle of their daily routines when, for some reason, the rhinoceros and the elephant began to fight

295

It started as a small scuffle but quickly escalated to a full-out animal brawl. Though the family did not know why it started, the baby elephant ventured too close to the rhinoceros' stall, and the rhino—not in a particularly good mood that day—kicked the baby back into its own stall. This angered its mother, which smacked its trunk into the rhino's backside. The rhino spun around and retaliated with a jab to the elephant. Then the fight ensued with ferocity.

The elephant reared up in its massive cage on its clumsy hind legs and kicked the rhino in the head. The rhino, now in a rage at this, smashed through the railing that separated the two stalls and slammed hard into the elephant, its horn passing only inches from the elephant's hide.

At this, the mate of both the elephant and the rhino ushered their young into the furthest corner of their respective stalls.

The animals on the bottom floor, where the rhino

and elephant were battling, panicked. Then the second level did too. The top level of the stalls did not seem too disturbed, only mildly unsettled at the commotion. The middle-level animals were more alarmed, as they started bouncing and running about their own stalls. The bottom level, however, began to become almost violent as the two massive creatures warred.

The elephant blasted a call through its trunk in anger and slammed its clumsy head into the rhino's side, sending it stumbling away. It crashed through another stall railing and stumbled back into the makeshift "pond" Noah had fashioned for all of the amphibious creatures.

The rhino charged in retaliation, ignoring the fleeing alligator in the water, which barely dodged its hoof. The rhino brought its horn up for a stab into its opponent's underbelly but fell short of its mark as the elephant dodged with a step back and slammed its trunk into the side of the rhino's face, sending the rhino stumbling sideways into the wall of the ark, its horn crashing through the ark's hull.

The rhino yanked its horn free from the hull of the ship and shook its head, ignoring the water spraying in from the freshly made puncture. This gave the elephant a chance to attack with a clumsy kick to the rhino's side. The rhino fell to its side, its horn plowing through the ark's hull again, right next to its previous puncture.

The rhino quickly retracted its horn from the hull, again ignoring the water pouring from now both holes in the ark's hull and regained its footing.

By this time, Ham, being the closest to the fight, reached the animals and attempted to stop the fight. It was a poor decision on his part to step in between the deadly creatures. The elephant slapped Ham away with her trunk, sending him splashing into the growing pond, with a surge of pain.

He recovered quickly as the rhino smashed, sidelong, with full force into the elephant, sending it stumbling sideways, itself.

At this point, the rest of the family reached the fight, watching in horror as the elephant recovered and successfully knocked the charging rhino down.

The rhino used its momentum as it fell to roll sideways, back onto its feet, managing to crash its horn into the flooring of the ark. Water erupted from the newly created puncture as the rhino rolled to its feet.

At this point, the family split into groups, Naomi, Noah, Shem, and Japheth worked to calm the rhino; and Mirriam, Zaphira, Ham, and Dinah worked to calm the elephant.

The eight managed to distract the two animals while the rhinoceros was recovering from a blow that sent it stumbling away from its foe.

The noise was deafening as the water rushed into the ship. The animals panicked, and the family screamed out in hopes to distract the two creatures from each other.

They eventually were able to lead the two deadly creatures to their families, which seemed to calm them even more.

Once the two animals seemed calm, Zaphira and Dinah began to calm the rest of the animals on the bottom level. The men frantically went about trying to plug the damning leaks. The water rushed in, rapidly filling up the bottom of the ark, and they all knew it was only a matter of time before the water filled the ark so much that it would sink. They all knew time was not on their side. The water rushed in, nonstop. To little avail, Shem put a hand over each of the two holes the rhino made in the wall, and Ham pressed his hands down on the hole in the floorboards, now submerged beneath the growing pool while Noah and Japheth frantically rushed to the cargo hold containing the spare pieces of wood.

Ham ignored the throbbing pain in his side, his adrenaline surging, and attention on the more immediate need to keep the boat afloat.

"I can't hold it!" Shem screamed. "It's too strong. Hurry!"

Noah and Japheth burst through the cargo hold door, Noah scrambling for the nails and hammers and Japheth snatching a couple short boards of wood. The two raced back down the stairs.

Noah and Japheth were almost to Ham and Shem when Noah tripped, slamming into the floor. The hammers and nails went flying. Japheth tumbled over his father, sending the wood clattering to the floor, as well. Neither took even a second to recover. They immediately jumped to their feet.

Noah frantically searched for the hammers, found them and snatched them up while Japheth hurriedly grabbed the boards, one of which was floating in the growing pool of ocean water.

"The nails!" Noah hollered. "Where are the nails?" he screamed as he scanned the floor. He saw one lying halfway into the pool and snatched it up. He jumped to his feet and handed a hammer to Naomi, who stood with the rhinos to keep them calm.

"Find the nails," he ordered, not waiting for a response.

Naomi immediately began scanning the ark floor for any of the nails. They were large, more like small spikes than nails, so she hoped they would not be that hard to find. Her eye caught a dark form in the pool of water.

"I found one!" she exclaimed. "Mirriam. Come get it," she shouted as she pointed toward the dark form. Mirriam quickly moved away from the elephants she and Zaphira were trying to calm. Following Naomi's direction, she found and snatched up the nail.

Noah and Japheth reached Shem first. Japheth dropped one of the boards so he could easily set the other lengthwise against the ark wall, hoping to cover both holes. Luckily it did. Japheth and Shem pressed the wood against the holes, leaning with all their might to keep the wood against the wall, struggling against the pressure of the water shooting from the holes.

Noah took the single nail and started hammering away between the two holes. He only hoped the holes were far enough apart not to cause a crack when he started hammering. If he did cause a crack, they wouldn't know. The nail went through in seconds, and the wood seemed easier to hold, but none dared shift their weight just yet.

Mirriam showed up with the second nail, then, and Noah snatched it out of her hands, barking another order for more nails. Merriam immediately went back to searching for another nail. The water was getting deeper now, and it wasn't as easy to see through the grime that was now floating on the water.

The family hadn't finished their chores, and the fecal matter that was not yet flushed into the sewage hold, along with food and whatever was loose in the vicinity of

303

the water, was floating around by now. Merriam dropped on all fours and started feeling around at the bottom of the pool.

"Hold the wood there. Don't let go!" Noah ordered to his sons and started blindly searching the sewage-filled water for the nails. Moments later, he found one, as did Mirriam.

Noah ordered Mirriam to get more nails from the storage hold and hammered the two nails into the board. She immediately darted off to fetch more nails while Noah hammered the two he had found into the wall. After Noah finished hammering the last two nails into the wood, he ordered his two sons to continue holding the wood and snatched up the other floating woodcut and moved to the hole Ham was uselessly trying to plug with his own hands. The two set the wood over the hole, and both knelt on it while they waited for the next nail. It was then that one of the alligators—forgotten about in the circumstances—

emerged with a nail in its jaws. Without hesitation, Noah snatched it out of the alligator's mouth and set about hammering under the water.

This particular hole was on the floor, so it was particularly difficult to hammer because it was harder to have force under the water, and it was hard for him to see. With great effort, Noah finally got the first nail in. By that time, Mirriam had returned with a handful of nails. He snatched the nails and told her to go get more wood as well.

Naomi and Zaphira ventured away from the deadly animals, keeping close attention to see if they started acting up again in all the commotion. After they noticed that the animals were remaining calm, they moved to help Mirriam and their husbands. Noah gave Naomi directions to get some pitch and heat it in the hearth. He ordered Zaphira to get several long beams and bring them to him.

With the nails all hammered in the first boards, the water was now merely a large trickle, rather than a bursting stream, which made everyone feel better.

Soon, the family had the newly "fastened" wood pieces somewhat secured, and they were working now on removing the water from the boat. They had taken several long beams and wedged them between the repaired holes above the water and an adjacent load-bearing beam that doubled as a stall pole, securing the wood piece against the wall, so they didn't have to hold it. They did the same with the wood under the water, but they wedged it between the hole and the walkway to the second floor. This gave the family time to seal the holes from leaking.

The women and Noah's children scooped the water up into barrels and hauled them up to the top deck to pour overboard. Noah, however, worked on sealing the boards covering the leaking holes.

He first slapped a heavy amount of heated pitch over the nails, so the nail holes were completely covered. Then he stuffed as much pitch as he could between the hull and the wood piece, hoping to seal the edges tight enough that no water would leak through.

The makeshift repair under the new pool of water was the difficult one. Noah had to wait until the water was hauled out and the area was clear to work without water to complicate things. Since the wood was not dry, it would take the pitch longer to dry anyway, and he wasn't sure how long it would hold.

The family had gotten most of the water out, and Noah was about to go up to the hearth to heat up more pitch when he was knocked off his feet, along with his entire family and most of the animals. The air around them erupted with the distinctive sound of wood scraping on rock, then the cracking and splintering, and finally shattering of wood. They felt the vibration through the floor. Whatever happened had definitely caused damage somewhere. Then, all was silent—except for the animals voicing their nervousness.

"What was that?" Japheth asked.

"Did we hit land?" Naomi asked. The family all looked at each other. Upon understanding that there didn't seem to be any more holes or leaks, they all anxiously made their way above deck.

They started out at a concerned jog, then a slight run, and finally a full sprint. When they got to the top deck and made it outside, they ran along the side of the boat until they saw it.

It wasn't land, but a jutting rock tip. The only reason they noticed it was because the water around it was clear and shallower than that of the rest of the ocean. They noticed the rock when they stopped looking further out from the ark and leaned over as they saw the shadow in the ocean. The rock had pierced the hull at the refuse hold, of all places.

"Well, that would be why we didn't see any leaks or holes," Shem commented.

"I'll go see how bad it is," Ham said. "We should probably not open the refuse hold until we know how much water we are taking on," he finished as he rushed to the gate for the external catwalk. The family nodded in agreement.

Ham quickly made his way down the walkway. It had seemed the sudden stop had scared away all of the occupants of the above deck and walkway. He neared the puncture and cautiously peered inside, not wanting to get any sewage on him, for at this point the water had filled up the hole and started escaping. A sudden breeze sent the foul smell of the refuse hold rushing into Ham's face, which almost cost him his balance.

"How's it look?" Zaphira asked.

"Well, it's already full to the hole, and coming out," he replied. Ham glanced around the area and noticed the rock curved under the ark and seemed to angle slightly downward for several dozen feet at which point he could no longer see the shadow in the water. He started back to the deck. "It looks like we're practically resting on this rock, or whatever it is," he reported. "It doesn't look like we will be in any trouble, but we should probably keep checking out here. But I don't think the water is higher than the refuse hatches on the middle level, so I think we're safe to open them."

The family nodded, and they headed back into the ark to try and finish the repairs to the cargo deck.

Soon, most of the water had been removed, and Noah was able to pitch the flooring. Though he knew it would take a tremendously long time to dry, he hoped it would work.

Over the next few days, Noah checked the pitch, and to his relief, it had worked as it should. The seal held firm.

A NEW WORLD

Again, things had leveled out to their monotonous norm, and the family kept about business as usual. Once their work was done, they enjoyed their free time, either together or separately. The jutting rock had slowly been rising—or rather the water had slowly been decreasing—and the family had begun to realize they were atop a mountain. The jutting rock was a corner tip of the mountain. The ark had indeed rested on a large formation, which they had started calling Ararat.

Two and a half months after they hit Ararat, they had started noticing more jutting rocks, or larger pieces of dry land, emerging from the water's surface, and in another month and a half, these tips became like icebergs protruding from the depths of the sea. The water was receding now, and the mountaintop growing larger out of the sea.

It was then that Noah decided to send out a raven. On the 263rd day, he stood out on the deck and waved the raven away. He figured if the raven came back, then it meant that it could not find a place to rest. If it didn't come back, then land was near. He hoped the raven wouldn't come back. He and his family were, indeed, tired of living on the boat.

Noah again stood out on the top deck of the ark. He worked on filling the basin of seawater so he could start distilling a new batch. It had been two weeks since he let the raven out, and one week since he had released the dove. It had only been a few hours, but if the dove flew as it and the raven before it had, it would soon return, like before. It disappointed him both times when the creatures of the air had returned mere hours after being released. He found himself constantly looking toward the direction in which he had released the dove. He had made it a point to start filling up the water basin when he was above deck waiting for the fowl to return.

When he saw the dove approaching, again, he was disappointed, yet not as much as the last two weeks. He must have been getting used to disappointment, he thought.

The dove landed on the rail and Noah noticed a leaf in the dove's beak. His heart skipped a beat as he saw the leaf. He held out his hand for the dove, and it landed on the back of his hand. Noah gently took the leaf and started toward the cargo decks, dodging those sea creatures who used the deck as a tanning bed.

He stopped suddenly as his hand touched the door handle to the living quarters.

His family was used to living on this ship, and he started thinking if everybody knew there might be land somewhere out there, they might all become impatient. It might make the rest of the time on this ship—however long it was—torture, knowing they might be able to leave soon, but not being able to just yet. Even just the fact of the birds returning disappointed him, he didn't want that for the rest of his family.

He turned around, somberly, and walked to the edge of the ark, releasing the leaf into the wind. The breeze snatched it up and flung it overboard. He watched it fall to the ocean and float away in the current.

At least he would be the only one tortured by the fact that there was land out there—somewhere. At least he could shield his family from weekly disappointment when the birds returned.

He hadn't yet told any of them that he had come out here and released the birds.

Ignorance is bliss, he thought and went back inside.

A week later, Noah sent the dove out again, but it never returned. This gave him hope that their time stuck on the ark was nearing an end. He did not know that end he longed for wouldn't come for over three more months.

Those last three months were dreadfully long for the family. They all knew the end of their imprisonment was near, and every day seemed to grow longer and more monotonous. Maybe it was because they could see a notable difference in the vast world changing before them. Every day, it seemed, the mountaintop they had run aground on revealed itself more and more, the jutting rock that penetrated the hull of their refuse compartment enlarging until it revealed itself to be a massive rock that had somehow been split down the middle and seemed to create a perfect cradle for the ark.

This cradle was the only reason the ark held upright. If this rock had not been shaped as it was, then as the water receded, the ship would have tipped to the side—and that would have been utterly disastrous.

Over the next thirty days, the water quickly receded, revealing a somewhat leveled out land mass a few feet lower than the jutting rock that cradled them. When Noah noticed this, he made a rope latter out of some spare rope in the cargo hold. All the family anticipated leaving the confines of the ship and had all had enough of the close quarters. They looked forward to living on the land again. The ladder had become their newest symbol of hope—their newest venture into the new world, and when Noah had finished the rope ladder, which didn't take long at all, they gathered on the upper deck, almost ceremonially and waited for Noah to secure the newest addition to their great ship.

"Okay," Noah said as he finished securing the rope and held the rope out, "who wants the honor of being the first person to step onto the new world?" Immediately, the three brothers reached out for the rope. Ham was just a hair faster than Shem or Japheth, and when he snatched the rope first, he let a grin of triumph, mixed with taunting, engulf his face as he dropped the rope ladder down the side of the ark.

The brothers jested with Ham about him taking such a long time to get down and shook the ladder periodically. Ham replied with a harsh look and angry comment.

Ham reached the last rung of the ladder, and the family hushed in anticipation.

"It still looks pretty muddy," Ham informed.

"Quit being a pansy, and step off, already. It's only mud!" Japheth hollered back.

Ham stepped out gently onto the muddy surface, slowly putting his weight onto the mud. His foot sank all the way down to his ankle, and just as he was about to pull his foot back up, it stopped sinking. He put his full weight on his foot, then, his grip still held tight on the ladder, and sank another inch. He stood on his one foot a moment, ensuring that he wouldn't sink anymore, and once he felt secure enough that he wouldn't sink further, he stepped out with his other foot.

"Hey, what's taking so long?" Shem hollered down. Ham looked up in irritation.

"You guys see how deep I sank here? You are more than welcome to come down here if you think I'm going too slow!" he yelled back.

The brothers laughed.

Now, with both feet sunk past the ankle, Ham let go of the rope ladder and began his short trek farther away from the ark. He felt the resistance of the mud that engulfed his foot as he pulled up, and the sucking sound as the mud released his feet left him uneasy. He made his way a few steps and yelled back as he started to turn around.

"It's ankle-deep and pretty hard to walk, but it doesn't seem so bad!" He felt himself sink a little more. He froze, realizing he had nothing to grab onto so far away from the ark.

"I just sank a little more!" he informed. A second later, he sank more, now down to his shins. He pulled his foot out of the mud, the sucking sound, now a symbol of danger in his mind. His next step sunk only ankle-deep to his relief and he quickly pulled his other leg out from its shin-high entrapment. As he pulled his second leg out, his first leg sunk to shin level, which caused him to lose his balance, and he prematurely dropped his leg, knee first, which sank, the mud engulfing his leg to mid-thigh, along with his entire lower leg. As this happened, his front leg sank more, as well, and he instinctively held out his hand to catch himself as if he were on solid ground. He immediately regretted this as his arm sank to the elbow.

Japheth immediately began laughing as he saw his brother fall into the mud. Shem, allowed himself a moment or two to laugh, but kept his demeanor less jovial, as he understood the possible danger his brother was in.

Ham tried to lift himself free, but the awkward position he found himself in: one leg buried past the knee, the other buried to the knee, and leaning to the side with an arm buried to the elbow, did not leave him much leverage or strength to be able to pull himself free.

"Uh, guys, I could use some help here. I am stuck."

Upon hearing his brother's confession, Japheth began a fresh wave of laughter. Shem, however, immediately began climbing down the rope ladder to help his brother. Noah and the others waited for Shem to attempt a rescue, knowing that too many people trying to help would cause more problems.

Shem reached the bottom rung of the ladder and hopped off, keeping a firm grip on the ladder, and sank shin deep into the mud. He plodded his way through the mud as far as the rope ladder would allow, which was only two steps. The ladder was stretched as far as it would stretch away from the ark. He was still several feet from his brother, and the two stretched as far as they could in an attempt to reach each other. Ham stretched his free arm as far as he could, which was not much due to his awkward position, but neither could stretch far enough to grab ahold.

"I have an idea," Noah hollered down and darted away. He came back a few moments later with a floor plank and tossed it overboard. The plank landed a few inches from Shem, sending an explosion of mud into the faces of both Shem and Ham. Shem maneuvered himself to grab the wood with his free hand, understanding what his father was thinking. He brought the floor plank between himself and Ham. Shem held one end, and Ham grabbed the other, as he, too, understood. Ham maneuvered his free arm around the plank so that he had a good grip, and he pulled with all his might, wiggling his trapped arm and legs as much as his awkward position would allow him. Finally, the mud released his arm with a sucking sound, and moments later, he was free of his prison. When Ham had trudged his way close enough to Shem, they dropped the plank and grabbed hands.

A few minutes later, both were climbing back up the rope ladder.

"Well, looks like we're stuck here for a while longer," Shem said as he pulled himself onto the deck.

***

Over the next two months, the family continued their chores and took time daily to venture to the deck of the ship to look out over the new world, their future home. It seemed that, even daily, the water continued to recede farther and farther away.

Some of the smaller, lighter-weight animals somehow found their way onto the muddy land. Weighing as little as they did the mud did not swallow them as it had Ham.

Over the last few months, several of the animals had given birth to little ones and had begun stretching the food resources very thin.

Two months after Ham's unsuccessful venture to the new world, the family was about their daily chores when a bright orange glow appeared along the side of the ark, illuminating the inside as if they were outside.

The family almost panicked at first, thinking that, somehow, the ark had caught on fire, until, after only a few seconds, the ark entrance fell outward with a loud creak and smash. Bright daylight erupted through the door, replacing the orange glow.

The family raced down to the lower level, all understanding with profound joy the implications of what had just transpired. They raced through the threshold and onto the dry ground. They all stood together, the ark to their backs and a void of dirt surrounding them on all other sides.

They could sense something was about to happen. They could feel something was happening. They felt it at their feet before they heard it. It took mere minutes, but they would never forget those minutes for as long as they lived.

They felt a slight shake, then heard a gentle rumble. They saw trees sprout just a few yards away and grow before their very eyes. They grew in moments. It started with a few, then more, and more, and more, until an entire forest had sprung up before them. When the trees were fully grown, the clearing of mud between them and the new forest grew grass in mere seconds.

"Come on!" Japheth ordered and ran back into the ark. The rest of the family followed a second later, not sure what he was doing, but they trusted in the excitement in his eyes.

They followed him up to the top floor and realized what he was thinking. He tore through the entrance to the living quarters and out onto the deck, the family following.

They were truly amazed at what they saw. As far as the eye could see, trees were still growing off in the distance. To the side was a massive body of water. Not too far off, behind them, was open grassland with bushes and smaller trees, and more trees on the opposite side of the ark.

They stood for long moments, just soaking up the view.

"Look," Zaphira said, pointing to the sky. They all saw a multicolored arch in the sky and gasped in amazement. A booming voice erupted, then, from everywhere, it seemed.

"I give you this sign as a remembrance of your journey and a promise that the world will never again be flooded, that you need not worry."

Eventually, after they had their fill of their newly created surroundings, the family started to let the animals out of their cages. The animals all quickly ventured out into the new world. Some stayed near the ark for a while, then migrated away. Others immediately ventured far from the ark, never to be seen by the family again.

The insects and other small creatures had taken it upon themselves to migrate before the family had ever started releasing the other animals. Lines of ants, spiders, snakes and other creatures littered the floors of the ark as they escaped the confines of the ship while flies, butterflies, bees and all sorts of flying insects buzzed overhead soaring toward freedom. Over the next few months and years, the family emptied out the stores of the ship, building new homes, gardens and equipment. When the stores were emptied, they began dismantling the ark itself, repurposing wood and other materials. Soon, they had started a new life—and made new additions to their family.

They had learned on the ark, and even more so now, that their world was, indeed, new. From the color of the sky to the drastically extreme temperature differences, they had to learn to adapt to this new way of life. The forest had exploded with life soon after the animals had left. It seemed the Creator had blessed all life to flourish in this new world.

The new world would be full of new experiences and adventures, they all knew.

Visit C. J. Korryn's website for more of his books.

https://www.cjkorryn.com/books

If you liked the book, please leave a review of the book on Amazon or the store website that you purchased the book on.

Connect with C. J. Korryn through:

Website:

https://www.cjkorryn.com

Blog:

https://authorcjkorryn.wixsite.com/blog

Facebook:

https://www.facebook.com/AUTHORCJKORRYN/

Instagram:

https://WWW.instagram.com/cjkorryn/

Serial novel subscription:

https://www.cjkorrynserialsubscriptions.com/

www.ingramcontent.com/pod-product-compliance
Lightning Source LLC
Chambersburg PA
CBHW070213260626
47160CB00002B/539